Three women so outrageous... they've got to be family.

MAGGIE: Her divorce is final. Her career in shambles. And now she's moving back in with her mama. But it's now or never if reliable Maggie is ever going to learn feisty Mama's secret to living life with courage, conviction...and laughter.

VICTORIA: There's no way a bit of heart trouble is going to get Mama down. She's lived her entire existence wearing red feathered gowns, dancing in the rain...and telling everyone exactly what she thinks.

JEAN: Suddenly faced with a late-in-life pregnancy, Jean's first reaction is to lean on Maggie. But maybe it's time to ditch her worries and find out how far her own strength—and family love—will take her.

Peggy Webb

Peggy Webb is passionate about books, music, theater, gardening, her family, her friends and her dog. When she's not writing, she's either clipping roses in one of the gardens she designed and planted, on stage at her local community theater in roles such as M'Lynn Eatenton in *Steel Magnolias*, singing in her church's choir, at her vintage baby grand playing blues, visiting children in far-flung places or laughing with friends. She also writes screenplays, serves on Tupelo's Film Festival committee and claims to make the best walnut bread in two states (MS and AL).

This native Mississippian launched her career with a book that hit number one on romance bestseller lists and earned her the Waldenbooks Bestselling New Author Award. Since then, her more than fifty novels have consistently appeared on bestseller lists and won national awards.

She shares her love of books with her students at Mississippi State University as well as lecture audiences throughout the U.S., and she shares her home with the perfect male—her dog.

PEGGY WEBB

Driving Me Crazy

Dear Reader,

My mother died the way she lived, with sass and courage. *Driving Me Crazy* is my memorial to her and my gift to you, the gift of Mama.

She is the only person I know who could become a character in a novel without embellishment. When my muse started whispering this book in my ear, Mama was right there, too, dictating and running the show, the way she always did.

To prove I was in charge, I gave her a dog, the biggest one I knew—my hundred-pound chocolate Lab, Jefferson. Of course novels are fiction, so I turned him into a golden retriever who couldn't hang on to his hair.

Now, before you start putting two and two together and getting sixteen, I have to set the record straight. I have two sisters, and neither one of them is Jean. Well...maybe there's a little bit of them in Jean. Both are great cooks, and my older sister, who lives nearby, often invites me to dinner. That's why *Driving Me Crazy* is dripping with butter. I got so hungry writing the scene about peach cobbler that I had to go into the kitchen and make one.

Is anybody else in this book real? Hmmm...maybe. But I'll never tell. I'll leave it to you, dear reader, to figure that out for yourself. So go to the kitchen, make a big peach cobbler and settle back for a funny and heart-touching read.

Oh, and please visit me at my Web site www.peggywebb.com. I do enjoy your company.

Peggy

P.S. Here's my peach cobbler recipe: Melt one stick of butter, the real kind, in a glass dish. Mix 1 cup each of sugar and self-rising flour, add ¾ cup of milk and pour this mixture into the butter. (Do not stir it in.) Scatter one can of sliced peaches, drained, over the batter and butter, then bake for thirty minutes at 350°F. Yum!

In memory of Mama who taught me to love books and music and flowers. Her independent nature, sharp intelligence, indomitable spirit and sassy ways color every page of this story, and my gratitude to her is infinite.

I don't know whether she put words in my mouth or I put words in hers. But this I know: somewhere she's smiling.

Acknowledgments

Eternal gratitude to Mama, who inspired this story, to my sisters, Jo Ann and Sandra, who lived it with me, and to all my dear friends who lifted me up when I forgot how to fly. Also a special thanks to my agent, Evan Fogelman, who is my biggest fan, and to Tara Gavin, long-time friend and mentor who welcomed me back into the fold.

CHAPTER 1

The weather will be mostly cloudy today with scattered thundershowers in the afternoon. Drivers, proceed with caution. Pay attention, now! I know what I'm talking about.
—*Joseph "Rainman" Jones, WTUP-FM Radio*

I'm driving along in a fog, which is my life in a nutshell.

A year ago when I divorced Stanley, I expected heroes to line up outside my door to worship at the shrine of my pot roast and my crotchless panties. What I got was one hot hunk who loved shrines but hated commitment and one geriatric who drooled his soup and peed on the toilet seat.

After I finally fled a marriage I couldn't fix, I saw my future self as happily re-wed, gainfully employed and skinny. I'm none of the above. What I am is forty-one and lost—in more ways than one—and even if I had a map, I couldn't see the road. Fog shrouds everything, including my Jeep, as I inch down what I hope is Highway 371 to rescue Mama.

That's me. Maggie Dufrane. Rescuer of stray cats, wounded dogs, latchkey kids, lonely old farts, sick neighbors and a seventy-five-year-old mama.

There ought to be a law against emergency phone calls at five o'clock in the morning, especially from my sister, Jean, who equates hangnails and bad haircuts with floods and tornadoes…and who feels compelled to ask my opinion about all of them.

Her alarmist viewpoint explains why I didn't bolt out of bed this morning when she wailed, "Maggie, you've got to come."

"Jean, do you know what time it is? This had better be good."

"It's Mama. She fell and banged her head. She called me a little while ago, *crying*."

Her words jolted me awake. Granted, Mama is feisty and dramatic. Once an actress, she's partial to histrionics that involve wild gestures, contorted features and a raised voice. But tears? Never!

I leaped from the covers, got tangled in the phone cord and fell in a heap with yesterday's sweatpants.

"What are we going to do, Maggie?" Jean blubbered.

Although she's two years older than I, she has been asking me that question all my life. She asked it thirty years ago when our Persian cat got stuck in a tree and wouldn't come down. She asked it when she leaned too close to the candles at her wedding rehearsal and her hair caught fire. She asked it when Daddy's pickup truck fell through the bridge and he floated to Glory Land on the Tombigbee River.

"Just hang on, Jean," I told her, as I have a thousand times. "I'll think of something."

And I will…the minute I assess the situation. I always do.

Right now, though, I'm concentrating on driving.

Today is Saturday, April fifteenth, my birthday. I hadn't planned to be a one-man cavalry. What I'd meant to do was ease out of bed around nine o'clock, indulge in a long bubble bath, then pamper myself with a leisurely breakfast of freshly squeezed orange juice and croissants with strawberry jam, alfresco. That means "on the fire escape" because my downtown Tupelo apartment building was once a department store whose owners had no need for balconies—and the current management considers adding them frivolous.

What I'm doing, instead, is charging forth in my ex-husband's once-white dress shirt, gray sweatpants cast off from yesterday's workout at Curves and red-sequined flip-flops, the only evidence of my plans for decadence and celebration.

As the clock inches toward six, the scattered patches of fog begin to lift and I can see the lake that borders Mama's north pasture. What if she's badly hurt? What will I do?

Though I pretend otherwise, I don't have all the answers. If I did, I'd have a house, a mortgage and a sex life. I'm not even close to having any of those things, which explains why I can be thrilled by the thought of a birthday celebration on a fire escape.

Alone, on the fire escape.

Now I've cracked open the door, and Depression pokes his giant foot through. The next thing I know he'll have his big hairy self sitting on the front seat, and then who will rescue Mama? Who will play taxicab driver for Jean, who backed Daddy's car over a hydrangea bush when she was fifteen and never saw the need to master reverse? Or forward, either, for that matter, especially after Mama said, "Let Maggie try it. She's efficient."

I switch away from the patter of Tupelo's most popular DJ, Joseph "Rainman" Jones, to a station that plays music, hoping to boost my spirits by warbling along to "Blue Eyes Crying in the Rain" with Willie Nelson. That's me, Miss Efficient and Cheerful. Reliable, too, the one you want to call when something goes wrong.

I peer into the lingering mists for any lurking hydrangea bushes or stray cattle that might waylay me. I'm in rural Mississippi now, the farm country of my childhood where haylofts know how to become castles and tree branches know how to become racehorses worthy of the Kentucky Derby.

Jean is waiting for me on Mama's front porch, her pink slacks inside out and her matching pink tennis shoes dew-soaked from the grassy pasture that separates her house from Mama's. Her blond hair sticks up like the feathers of baby birds as she rushes toward me.

"Mama's got the dead bolts on. I can't get in."

"Where is she? Can you see her?"

"No, but I can hear her moaning."

I rattle the front door and yell, "Mama! Mama, can you hear me?"

"Ohhh. Ohhhh." Mama is either gasping her last breath or auditioning to be a ghost for Halloween. With her, it's hard to tell. Once, when she was recovering from the flu, she telephoned at 6:00 a.m. to say I had to hurry right over, it was an emergency. On the drive I imagined finding her relapsed and half-dead. She was dying, all right, she said, from starvation, but didn't feel like frying the bacon herself.

Now panicked, Jean races around the house to scope the south side while I jerk screens off the front porch windows and shove against casements to see if one of them can be opened without breaking the glass.

"Maggie, around here. Quick."

"What?" To save time I jump off the side of the porch, but the dew-slick grass outsmarts me and I meet the damp ground with a thud. Jean grabs my arm and hauls me up.

"Hurry. You've got to climb through that window." She points to a south-facing window with a narrow slit at the bottom where it's not quite connected to the sill.

"You're shorter, Jean. I'll hoist you up."

"If you think I can get my forty-five-inch butt through that thirty-six-inch opening, you're crazy."

I'm not about to admit the size of my hips, so I step into Jean's cupped hands, grab hold of the windowsill and then…nothing.

"You can do it, Maggie. Come on. Heave-ho!"

"I'm heaving, I'm heaving."

Inside, Mama's still moaning. And now, so is Jefferson, the ten-year-old golden retriever who is her companion, her watchdog and her best friend. If this were the movies, he'd be trained to open the door with his mouth and swab her forehead with a wet washcloth clutched in his paw.

Who am I kidding? If this were the movies, I'd re-write the ending. Heck, I'd rewrite the middle, too. Instead of teetering on the windowsill over a thorny lantana with rescue on my mind, I'd be on a yacht in the Mediterranean with my rich husband, the Duke of Somewhere Important, with *something else entirely* on my mind. Food, if you want to know the truth, which just goes to show the alarming shifts that come with a certain age. What I'm thinking about is having a personal chef who hand-feeds me squab and pears glazed with honey.

"She's dying in there." Jean destroys my honey-glazed vision. "You've *got* to climb in and get her."

"Where's Walter when we need him?" Jean's husband, who works for an international environmental company, puts together deals to convert garbage to usable goods. His sumo-wrestler looks and teddy-bear personality make him hugely popular and successful.

"He had to fly to Japan yesterday. *Hurry*, Maggie." Jean puts her weight behind me and I catapult sideways into the lantana.

"Oh, lord, you're going to end up in the hospital with Mama."

"I am not. If you'll just stop wringing your hands and give me another boost, I'm going through that window."

Jean starts praying, and this time I get through, thanks to guts and grace.

Mama is stretched out on the floor with Jefferson lying beside her, his big head pillowed on her chest. They both raise their heads at the same time.

"What took you so long?" Mama says. The skin on her forehead is peeled back to the bone and blood is caked around the gaping wound. My knees feel wobbly and my stomach churns. The only thing that saves me is Mama.

"Don't just stand there," she snaps. "Help me up from here. I've got to go to the doctor."

The thing about Mama is that she's going to take charge, no matter what. When the time comes, I can imagine her sitting up from her casket saying, "Fluff up this pillow, it's hard as a brickbat. And for Pete's sake, go out and buy yourself a new dress. I don't want any daughter of mine looking tacky at my funeral."

Now I ask her, "What happened, Mama?"

"I was feeling funny and when I tried to call Jean I fell and couldn't get up, that's all."

Pacemaker, I think. I've seen her get weak when her pacemaker needs adjusting—a simple procedure, thank goodness—done with computers.

I let Jean in, and she starts flapping around like a bird with a broken wing. How I'll ever get all three of us to the emergency room at North Mississippi Medical Center is a mystery to me.

"Can you walk?" I ask Mama.

"Don't be ridiculous. Of course I can."

We help Mama to the car, and up close I see that the wound is not as serious as it looks. What bothers me most is that Mama couldn't get up when she fell. And, by the way she winces when she walks, I suspect there's more going on than meets the eye.

We ensconce her in the back seat on a blue blanket and two pillows we grabbed on the way out the door, and while I drive, Jean bargains with God.

"If you'll just let us get Mama to the hospital safe and sound, I'll lose ten pounds. I swear."

Mama rises from her pillow-throne and snaps, "Can't you think of something less trivial, Jean? This is a life-and-death situation here."

"More like a three-ring circus," I say, and Jean giggles.

Laughter through tears. It's the Southern way, especially with women. I've spent my life watching Mama and her sister, Aunt Mary Quana, spin daily tribulations into stories with a touch of humor. They even did it with tragedy. After Daddy died, I asked Mama how she could still find anything to laugh about and she told me, *It's the only way to reduce pain to something manageable and render it bearable.*

The hospital looms ahead and it's a relief to turn Mama over to the experts, who rush out with a gurney and a mouthful of reassurances.

"Don't worry about a thing." The intern who takes charge is fresh-faced and his forearms are dotted with red-gold freckles that match his hair. I have sneakers older than he is. If I'd been lucky enough to have children, one of them might have looked like him. "You two go on and fill out the admission papers. We'll take good care of your mother."

I believe him, partly because of his earnestness, but mostly because it's the only way I can keep walking. *Just put one foot in front of the other,* I tell myself.

It takes thirty minutes and two college degrees, mine and Jean's, to figure out the forms. When we finally find a seating area to wait in while Mama gets her X-rays, we sink into the hard plastic chairs as if we're way past our prime instead of women who still have a little fire in the belly as well as other parts of the anatomy.

Well, occasionally, we do.

"I'm so tired of being Joshua," Jean says, as if she'd fought the battle of rescuing Mama all by herself.

"I'm tired of being Job."

"If it's not one thing it's another. What's happening with your book contract?"

"I haven't heard anything yet. My editor's had my new proposal only two weeks. She's in L.A. now visiting friends. I expect to hear from her as soon as she returns to New York."

"I hope so. How long has it been since your last contract? Eight months?"

"Nine. It's my fault, though. I lost my writing steam after the divorce and I'm just now getting it back."

Jean shifts in her chair, plants her tiny size-five feet side by side and picks at a hangnail. "Why don't they put cushions in these chairs? It's not enough that we're worried to death, we have to be uncomfortable, too. Maggie, you ought to write a letter."

She thinks I can fix anything. I guess it's because I always try.

But if I write any letters it's going to be to Shelia Cox, my editor. I'm a novelist with eight mysteries to my credit. Granted, I'm no Agatha Christie, but I was making enough money before I left Stanley to believe that I could support myself as long as my tastes matched my pocketbook. Translated, that means I won't be dashing off to Paris in a full-length mink. Of course, I wouldn't buy a mink even if I could afford one. I love animals too much to drape their poor little lost hides over my body. Paris, however, is a whole 'nother story.

What I ought to do is call Shelia. It's unlike her to take so long on one of my proposals, and it's certainly not like me to dither around with my hands tied while my career hangs in the balance. I blame this strange malaise on the divorce. It wasn't messy or recriminatory or protracted; Stanley and I are far too civilized for that. But no matter how strongly you believe that you must make a change, wrenching yourself out of a safe and familiar way of life is akin to pulling up anchor and setting sail over unfamiliar waters without a compass.

A nurse in crepe-soled shoes wheels Mama into the visiting area, and Jean and I move to either side of the gurney to hold her hands. With a huge bandage swathing her forehead and bruises on her arms where they drew blood, she looks pale and extremely fragile, not like the woman who could take Hannibal's place and single-handedly march an army with African war elephants across the Rhône River and over the Alps.

"The head gash is not serious, but she has a perforated ulcer," the intern tells us. For the first time I notice his name tag—Jake Brown. "A part of the aging process is that the body's organs become leaking, rusty pipes. Anything can go wrong. We're going to have to do emergency surgery."

"You can talk to me," Mama says. "I'm not dead yet."

Dr. Brown pats her hand. "Mrs. Lucas, my major concern is not the surgery itself but the complications that could arise because of your heart."

"I'm not *that* old."

"No, you're in remarkably fine shape, but your heart is beginning to wear out in ways your pacemaker won't help. Right now it's pumping at only thirty-three percent capacity."

"What does that mean?" I ask.

"Congestive heart failure."

His news sucks the wind out of Jean and me, but while she sinks into a chair and begins to cry without sound, I remain upright. Somebody has to.

Dr. Brown explains what this previously undiagnosed condition means—a gradual failure of the heart, which could wear out in one to seven years, and oxygen-starved body parts that give up bit by bit. Mama's lips tighten into a thin line, a certain sign that she's not fixing to roll over and play dead.

"Mrs. Lucas, the bottom line is that if we don't operate immediately, this perforated ulcer will kill you, but if we do, the surgery might also kill you."

"Wheel me out and cut me open. Everybody has to die of something."

I squeeze her hand and hang on, reluctant to let her go. Fighting back tears I tell her, "Mama, I love you."

"Maggie…" Mama's never been one to wallow in sentiment, but her eyes are watery so I brace myself for an amazing turnaround, a sort of death-bed confession of undying affection. "Jefferson will get nervous and lose all his hair if he has to sleep by himself. If I live through this and find him bald, I'm going to kill you."

So much for maudlin sentimentality. As the orderly races down the hall behind the gurney bearing Mama toward possible death, the little girl in me cries because Mama didn't wrap her arms around me and cling, but the rest of me braces up—which is exactly what Mama intended.

"Let's find the waiting room," I tell Jean.

The awful thing about waiting in hospitals is that they are so huge it takes fifteen minutes to get from anywhere to the cafeteria, and that's if you don't get lost. Although I'm the official driver for this family, my sense of direction is not much better than Mama's. She stopped driving two years ago when she left her glasses at home, mistook Horton Grimes's garden for the road to Burger King and ended up mowing down a row of cabbages and three rows of corn before he could stop her.

Two other people are in the surgery waiting room, a rawboned young man with straw-colored hair holding the hand of a girl in pink hair ribbons and a pink maternity top. She looks as if she ought to be playing dolls. They're bending toward each other whispering. I want to pat them both on the head and tell them everything's going to be all right.

I want to pat myself on the head and say the same thing.

"Maggie, I'm starving." Jean whispers, too, as if a normal voice might disturb a sleeping monster in this room that would rain disaster over our heads. "There's a vending machine down the hall," she adds. "Do you have any change?"

The machine offers an array of chips plus crackers spread with peanut butter and cheese, which would provide a bit more sustenance than Snickers bars and M&M's, but I go straight for the chocolate. After losing eight quarters, I draw back and give the machine a good kick. My reward is the blessed thud of candy hitting the tray.

I trot back into the room with my loot and hand Jean a Snickers. We tear into our candy then lean our heads against the wall as we close our eyes and work our jaws.

Suddenly Jean bolts upright. "Oh, lord, today's your birthday! I've got you a present."

"What is it?" I can't abide surprises. I've always been the kind of person who wants to know exactly what's going on and what to expect. When Jean and I were children, I would search the closets until I found our Christmas presents, then carefully tear back a corner of the wrappings to see what I was getting. I didn't rip into Jean's, though; she loves to guess.

"Well, if you must know it's a T-shirt with spangled printing on the front that reads Fifty and Foxy."

"I'm not fifty. Why didn't you get one that said forty?"

"They were out of the forties. Anyhow it's the foxy part that counts."

"You've got that right!"

Jean looks at me and we start laughing so hard we end up leaning against each other, crying.

My sweatpants are covered with grass stains, the knee sports a hole from the battle with the lantana and brambles are tangled in my mussed red hair.

The young couple sitting across from us moves two chairs down to get out of the path of the two wild and crazy women.

I send them a little smile to show we haven't entirely lost our minds. I want to straighten the young woman's now-lopsided pink hair ribbon, brush the young man's lank blond hair out of his eyes and say, *Listen, when you get older you'll understand.* You'll realize that it's what's inside that matters—the tough, resilient fiber that wouldn't let Mama fold under news of a failing heart, the faith that gave Jean enough strength to boost me over the windowsill, the courage that kept me driving when all I wanted to do was sit in a corner and weep.

I have more to celebrate than a birthday.

The announcement over the intercom gut-punches Jean and me: *Code blue! Code blue!*

I stiffen and squeeze my purse till the sides cave in. That's the way I always take bad news—with a tightened-up body that hides the way my insides turn to glass and explode into little shards that rip at my heart.

Jean, however, is a different story. Her entire body goes into overdrive, and the rest of her Snickers bar flies into the air when she jumps out of her chair to start pacing. "Ohmigod, Maggie, it's Mama, I just know it's Mama."

"We don't know that, Jean. Sit down and try to relax."

"The surgery's killed her. What are we going to do?"

The first thing I have to do is get her back into her seat before she stampedes the big-eyed couple. I jump up, grab hold of her and half drag her back to the chair. "Calm down, Jean. What we're not going to do is alarm the entire county."

I'm stroking her shoulders while I talk, and finally I feel the tension easing out of her. "Okay, now?" She nods, then huddles into a little ball, which means it's safe for me to retrieve the sticky wad of chocolate that landed in the doorway.

I bend down with the intention of scooping it up quickly and tossing it into the garbage can, but the candy's stuck to the floor.

"Excuse me."

Oh, even *worse*.

The deep male voice is the kind that usually goes with the body of a drop-dead gorgeous hunk, and naturally I'm still upside down, the best part of me facing the floor and the worst part facing *the voice*. I creak slowly upward trying to act as if the hips I'd had saluting the breeze still fit into size-six slacks.

"Are you with the Lucas family?"

I wish I could say no. I wish I could say, "We officially had our name changed last year. You have the wrong people."

But what I wish most of all is to have Mama standing by my side saying, "Don't just stand there, young man. Spit it out. I can take it."

Jean's crying again and so am I, but my sorrow is trapped inside where the tears don't show. Outside I'm a woman with straight back and upright chin, patting my sister's arm and saying, "Hush, Jean. We will survive this, too."

CHAPTER 2

Don't expect the sunshine anytime soon. This bad weather has set in for a while. There are smashups on Main and Church. Are you paying attention out there, drivers? The body count's rising, and I don't want it on my conscience.

—*Rainman*

The wheels of my Jeep swish against the pavement, whispering prayers of thanksgiving, *Mama's not dead, Mama's not dead*. She's in intensive care, though, hooked up to life-support machines that are doing the work for her worn-out body until she catches on and jerks out the tubes and yells, "Get me out of this place."

During the brief visitation allowed family, Jean and I stood on either side of her bed while I urged, "Come on, Mama. You can do it. You can beat this thing."

Her heart stopped during surgery, but the doctors got

it started again. "Before there was brain damage," the delicious-looking surgeon who'd had a close-up-and-personal view of my oversize backside had told us.

Alas, he's married. I always look at the ring finger. You never know.

Anyhow, I hope he's right. I can't imagine Mama without her sharp mind. I can't imagine life without Mama's pointed comments and razor-edged observations. But these are things I don't tell Jean as I drive down Gloster Street looking for a place to eat.

Both of us are starving. It's 2:00 p.m., and we've missed both breakfast and lunch. Not that it will hurt us. Jean calls the twenty-five pounds she needs to shed ten, and I call my excess "a little fluff."

"How about Lolly's Health Food Café?" I suggest. "We could get salads."

"Salads, my foot. I need comfort food. Butter and French sauces made with real cream and desserts loaded with nuts and ice cream and fudge topping."

"Sounds great. Mama pulled through. Let's celebrate," I say, and then I address Rainman via the radio. "You can predict storms all you want. I'm not letting you rain on my parade."

I pull into Ruby Tuesday and we sprint toward the restaurant without slickers and umbrellas, shivering in an unusually cold rain that came out of the blue. April

27

in Mississippi is like that, sometimes sending the bite of winter through our bones. Mother Nature loves to take Southerners by surprise, shake us out of the complacent notion that summer is just on the heels of blooming iris and azaleas, forsythia and verbena.

Inside, Jean and I order everything on the menu that's fattening.

"When life is shitty be good to yourself," Jean says. "That's my motto."

The butter I spread on hot rolls thaws my ice-cold feet; the steak smothered in onions, mushrooms and cheese warms my heart; and the double-fudge brownie with cherries and whipped cream reaches out and wraps its arms around me.

There's a lot to be said for Jean's theory. I think I'll subscribe to it. At least for today. At least for my birthday.

Jean had asked the waitress to put a candle on my double-fudge brownie. "Blow out the candle and make a wish, Maggie."

I grab her hand and say, "Wish with me, too, Jean. That makes it more powerful."

We close our eyes and imagine Mama sitting up in her narrow hospital bed demanding to know what she's doing hooked up to all that junk and why her daughters aren't there.

"I'm spending the night in the intensive-care waiting room," Jean says, as if she's reading my thoughts.

"The nurses said they'd call if there was any change."

"I don't care what they said. That's not the way Victoria Lucas's family does things. I'm staying."

The Lucas stubborn streak runs a mile wide through this family. I'm not fixing to try to argue with Jean, although I'm the one driving her around.

Sometimes being the only driver (except Walter, of course, who is hardly ever home) gets complicated. Take today, for instance. In addition to my madcap race from my apartment to Mama's and back to the hospital, I must now take Jean back to the hospital then return to my apartment for a toothbrush and pajamas before going to the farm to keep Mama's nervous dog happy.

It's not the spend-the-night party I'd imagined for my birthday.

By the time I finally get back home, it's dark. The fifteen marble stairs leading to my second-floor apartment feel like a hundred and fifteen. Aching bones I never knew I had, I mutter, "I might as well live in my car." I could keep my toiletries and pillow in the back seat and get a hot plate that plugs into the cigarette lighter. I could name the Jeep something cute like Rover and teach it to come when I whistle.

"Well, hello there, gorgeous! Where have you been all my life?"

Oh, lord, it's Newton Cramer, my landlord and across-the-hall neighbor, leering at me from the top of the steps. He says the same thing every time he sees me, and then giggles as if he's just thought of the world's most clever come-on. If Newton weren't as old as God, I'd take offense.

Instead I take pity. There he stands in slacks so big they'd fall off if he didn't wear red suspenders—or yellow, depending on his mood—and wingtip shoes that date back to the days before indoor plumbing.

"How are you, Newton?"

"Fine as cat's hair and fit as a fiddle."

"Well, don't take any wooden nickels."

Using hackneyed phrases is a snap for me because I taught high-school English for ten years and spent most of that time trying to get my students not to use them. My comeback makes Newton slap his knee with delight.

If Stanley had been that easy to please, we'd still be married. But my husband, a CPA, was a stickler for perfection. He kept tallies on everything—the number of times I bought chuck when he wanted Boston butt, the number of times I forgot dental appointments (even when I forgot them on purpose), the number of times I put the toilet paper on so that it rolled under instead of over, which is the way he considered correct.

Now, nobody tells me what to do except Mama, and that's not out of any desire to turn me into her concept of the perfect woman but out of her innate ability to dictate. Mama always stands her ground and rules every bit of the ground she stands on. With her gone, even temporarily, I feel as if I'm treading quicksand.

Ordinarily I'd pause on the steps long enough to chat with Newton, whose daughter lives in Trenton, New Jersey, and only calls on his birthday and the major holidays. But today is turning into the longest day of my life, and I need some time to hoist myself out of quicksand before I take on a neurotic dog that can't hold on to his hair in a crisis.

My apartment seems emptier than usual. Pristine. Not a throw pillow out of place, not a book or a magazine scattered about, not even a dust ball under the sofa. And certainly no cat hair and dog dander. No pets allowed in this building. No messy barking and mewing and racing down the fire escape to the back alley for a midnight potty break.

It looks as if nobody lives here, and maybe nobody

does. Maybe the spontaneous Maggie Dufrane I once was vanished after I left my husband, who'd forgotten how to hug, and my six-year-old cocker spaniel, who knew about everything but wasn't allowed in my get-away cocoon. Maybe my ghost took up residence inside apartment six of the Skylofts in downtown Tupelo, Mississippi.

Right now I can picture Jean curled into Mama's fuzzy blue blanket in a corner of the ICU waiting room talking to Walter on the phone, and he's reaching across continents to take her worries and put them on his own broad shoulders. She's crying—I know this without seeing, because she always does—and he's calling her *sweetie* and *baby*, making her feel cherished and protected and not quite so afraid.

I think I read somewhere that people who are in a stable, loving relationship live longer than singles who struggle along taking care of every little thing, including faucets that start dripping at midnight when you've finally conquered insomnia, and toilets that overflow just as you race toward the door, already late for church.

If what I read is true, then Jean will live to be a hundred and ten and I'll die next Tuesday.

Maybe if I call Stanley for a little sympathy—which he will most certainly give because he loves Mama—I'll prolong my life till a week from Friday. But somehow that's like admitting defeat. A call to my ex-spouse when I'm feeling vulnerable is practically saying, "I can't make it without you."

And of course I can. I miss the comfort of arms around me when I fall asleep, and I miss my little dog with his cold nose and messy ways, but I sure don't miss the feeling of always being a little inadequate, of never quite measuring up.

Stanley had a way of making the words *Maggie, if you were more organized, I'd be able to find my gray socks* sound as if I had single-handedly destroyed the institution of marriage.

Not that I was blameless, mind you. I had my own methods of inflicting small, daily wounds.

The day I first saw my name on the cover of a mystery novel, I was enormously proud. So were Jean and Mama. My sister sent roses, and Mama brought a German chocolate cake she'd baked, and we sat in the sunshine in my butter-yellow breakfast room eating huge slabs of cake, drinking French vanilla coffee from gold-rimmed china cups and celebrating.

All Stanley did was say, "I hope you know what you've gotten yourself into, Maggie."

"I do," I told him. "I've transformed myself from Stanley Dufrane's boring wife into a woman reviewers call the next Anne George…. Not that you care."

The crumbling of a marriage is never pretty and it's never fast. Although we didn't call each other names or engage in the sort of domestic brawls that alert neighbors and make the dog hide under the bed, we gradually changed from a couple sharing a life to two people living under the same roof, taking pains to avoid each other in the bathroom and to hide behind the newspaper at meals.

Finally I said to my husband, "I'm leaving. You can keep the house."

Not that I'm foolishly generous, but I just couldn't imagine Stanley living anywhere except the split-level ranch with the big oak tree in front and the John Deere lawn mower in the garage waiting for him to perform the first rites of spring: suit up, power up and roar! On the other hand, the house had become polluted for me, a place where accusations had settled into cracks in the ceiling tiles and recriminations lurked in corners to waylay me every time I entered the room.

Now I enter my cool, quiet bedroom with its blue-sprigged wallpaper and old-fashioned ceiling fan and breathe. Simply breathe.

The peace settles around me. The loneliness, too.

The hardest thing was not leaving the house but leaving the dream of happily-ever-after. I know, *I know*. Nobody believes in Cinderella with her Prince Charming anymore. It's all *Sex and the City*, and how many ways women can turn themselves into tough-talking, love 'em and leave 'em creatures who would be men except for high heels and push-up bras.

If I could rewrite the script, I'd restore grace and femininity. I'd make charm sexier than sassy retorts and striving for excellence more laudable than stepping over maimed cohorts to get to the next rung on the corporate ladder.

I am a dinosaur in the age of sleek, quick lizards.

I pack the things I'll need while I dog sit for Mama: pajamas, a change of clothes, toiletries, perfume. Why not? A little spritz of Jungle Gardenia always makes me feel like a powerful, sexy woman, somebody with a closetful of black lace and men languishing on the streets because I haven't yet returned their calls.

Oh, yes. A good book. A historical romance by Donna Fletcher. A delicious escape into a world of dashing Highlanders and the smart, feisty women who bring them to their knees with desire.

And that's all. I pack light because that seems hopeful, a sign that Mama will come blazing back to demand the latest *New York Times* crossword puzzle book, which is how she keeps her mind so sharp, and command the Lucas girls to shape up, which is easy if Victoria is telling you what shape to take, but seems impossible when her voice is stilled and the choices confusing.

The phone rings and when I pick it up, I notice the red light blinking on my answering machine. I'll listen to the messages later.

"Maggie…"

"What is it, Jean? Is it Mama?"

"I don't know. She looks awful. I just went in for visitation, and she didn't even squeeze my hand. I think she's dying."

Mama wouldn't die on my birthday. She's too strong-willed for that. Besides, I have to consider the source. This is my melodramatic sister talking.

"What do the nurses say?"

"They say she's stable, everything looks good."

"Okay. Great. You just hang in there tonight and I'll see you in the morning."

"Walter said he'd fly home if he needed to. I said I'd ask you if he should."

Oh, lord. Why me?

"Tell him to wait, Jean. I don't think it's going to be necessary."

After I hang up the phone, I punch the new message button and hear my editor's voice, sounding faraway and scratchy. I need a new answering machine.

"Hi, Maggie. It's Shelia. Call me. I have great news."

I dial her cell phone, expecting to get her voice mail, but it's Shelia I get.

"Maggie…I wanted you to be the first to know—I met someone in California."

"That's great," I tell her, meaning it. She's thirty-three, generous-hearted and lovely, and if anybody deserves somebody wonderful, it's Shelia.

"It is. He's a landscape architect, and his gardens are an absolute dream. You'll have to come out and visit us."

The bottom drops out of my stomach. "Come out? You're staying in California?" I have to sit down. Losing a good editor is like losing a good husband.

"Yes, but I don't want you to worry. Your manuscript is in the hands of Janice Whitten, and I know she'll love your work as much as I do."

I'm numb, and it's not until after we say goodbye that the questions and nightmare imaginings begin.

Who is Janice Whitten? Somebody new, for Pete's sake. Somebody who will loathe the idea of a slightly old-fashioned sleuth who revels in discovering rare books, tending her six cats and finding out whodunit to the dead bodies that keep cropping up in her bookstore. Somebody who hates grits and has never heard of fried green tomatoes. Somebody who won't know Maggie Dufrane from Adam's housecat.

God, I've turned into Newton. All I need is a pair of baggy pants and red suspenders. Of course, I'm already halfway there.

I strip out of my sagging sweatpants and Stanley's battered shirt and reach into my closet for jeans.

The phone rings again. It's Jean.

"Hey, I forgot to give you your birthday present."

"That's all right."

"Happy birthday, Maggie."

There was nothing happy about it. But what did I expect—a woman born on the anniversary of the sinking of the *Titanic?*

I hang up the phone and sit on the edge of the bed to put on sneakers. Sturdy shoes that say this woman means business. No sinking into the Atlantic for her. She's steady, upright, ready to plow ahead and go places.

The first place I have to go is the farm. And fast. It's already nine o'clock and Jefferson will be leaning against the kennel fence moaning.

I grab my overnight bag and my car keys.

Who knows? Maybe Janice Whitten is from Georgia and can't wait to buy my manuscript and share her grandmother's recipe for chess pie.

I hope it has lots of butter.

CHAPTER 3

When it rains it pours. The streets are slippery tonight, folks. If you're walking, don't fall. If you're
driving, don't skid into a ditch.
—*Rainman*

"**If** only you knew, Rainman. I skidded into the ditch
about the time Mama was hauled off to surgery three
years ago for her pacemaker. Or was it a year before
when it became obvious I no longer had a marriage
worth keeping?"

Here I am in the car, talking to the weatherman.
He's driving me crazy. Or maybe it's Jean and Mama.
Or my ex-editor and my ex-husband. Take your pick.

In the glow of the dashboard lights, I watch the
odometer click off the miles—129,201. My Jeep is only
six years old, which means I've traveled nearly ten
thousand miles per year more than average. That

39

would sound exciting if I'd actually been going places such as Savannah, Georgia, to eat fresh crab cakes and walk along beaches in red-gold sunsets, or Hot Springs, Arkansas, to plump up my wrinkles in the spas and go to the racetrack to root for a three-year-old filly named Lucky Lady.

Stanley and I went to Hot Springs on our honeymoon. We stayed at the Arlington and listened to the band play "Moon River" while a sleek, dark man with a handlebar mustache and shifty eyes danced with a white-haired woman wearing a rhinestone tiara and pink chiffon. We were there a week and she came every night, always wearing pink chiffon, always smiling while she danced. On Saturday night when Andy Williams was there to perform his signature song, she closed her eyes and sang along with him.

"Who is she?" I asked our waiter.

"Miss Gracie Smallwood," he said. "Her engagement party was here in this very ballroom in 1942, and when her fiancé didn't come back from the war, she kept coming here dressed in pink chiffon. She loves to dance. Sometimes when nobody will dance with her, she dances alone."

I think about Miss Gracie Smallwood as I drive down Highway 371 in the glow of a yellow moon that popped full-blown from beneath the clouds after the rains stopped and the night crickets started singing. With my window down so I can hear their song and smell the rich fecundity of freshly washed spring earth, I think about the tragedy of dancing alone.

And the promise.

There was something hopeful about Miss Smallwood's pink chiffon, something so full of grace and yearning that after I park the Jeep under Mama's magnolia tree and retrieve Jefferson in all his tail-wagging glory from the kennel, I ramble through Mama's huge stack of tapes until I find one that features Andy Williams singing his greatest hits. This takes a while. Mama's a collector, and her tapes, like everything else in this house, have overflowed their original space and leaked onto adjoining surfaces. In this case, they've spilled off the bookshelves into two hand-crafted wicker baskets.

While "Moon River" fills Mama's overstuffed bedroom, I twirl around bumping into furniture, the only girl in Mooreville who ever flunked Miss Femura Wright's after-school dance class, but dancing anyway, all these years later, dancing because it's better than crying.

Jefferson lies down and puts one paw over his eyes, too embarrassed to watch.

Or maybe he's just missing Mama.

I would miss her, too, if she weren't in every crack and crevice of this house. Two walls are covered with her collection of Japanese fans, eighty-five of them clinging to the yellow Sheetrock like brightly colored butterflies, the largest one spread above her headboard in a five-foot display of dripping cherry blossoms, red pagodas and doe-eyed young women in purple silk kimonos. A glass-front display case in the corner groans under the weight of 110 porcelain dogs, acquired one by one over the years with the same relentless zeal Mama uses in all her pursuits.

I remember ten years ago, when we were in San Francisco for my first book conference, and she wouldn't leave Chinatown until we found somebody who would open his shop after hours to sell her a miniature jade Foo dog she'd seen in the window.

Jefferson lifts his big head, ears pricked and tail thumping while the glass in the front door rattles.

Goodness, somebody's breaking in and Mama's fearless watchdog is fixing to lick him to death. I freeze in midpirouette and rack my brain trying to think up a weapon.

The door rattles again, followed by banging and the sound of a male voice. "Maggie! Maggie, is that you in there?"

Horton Grimes. The neighbor whose cabbages

Mama inadvertently harvested with the bumper of her car. He's been her slave ever since, with the full blessing of his wife, Miss Hattie.

I turn down the music, then skirt through the hallway being careful not to knock over Mama's fifty handmade pottery angels on whatnot shelves and her collector's cups from every state plus the Virgin Islands.

It has started to rain again and, when I open the door, Horton Grimes is huddled against the blowing moisture. I feel sorry for him. Besides, he's company at a time I suddenly realize I need to hear the sound of another human voice.

"Mr. Grimes. Come in."

"I saw your headlights over here earlier this morning while I was at the barn. Then when you came back a while ago, I said to my wife, Hattie, 'There's something wrong over to Victoria's house. I'd better go check it out.'"

In the dim yellow bulb of Mama's front-porch light, he looks jaundiced and slightly disreputable, his circa-1950s felt fedora at odds with his denim overalls that smell of sweet clover hay and barnyard fertilizer. The scent of his farm follows him through the door, and Jefferson runs around him in excited circles, sniffing, while I surreptitiously check the floor.

Is that a clump of hair? The lighting in Mama's house is bad, and with Horton standing there, I can't bend over to see.

I put my hand on Jefferson's collar to hold him still, but even standing by my side, he shivers and his sleek coat ripples like waves in the wake of a small racing craft. The next thing you know, I'll have to be driving him to appointments with his own psychiatrist.

Keeping him on a short leash, I lead Jefferson along with Mr. Grimes into Mama's living room, which has too many chairs for its size, inadequate lamps whose main function is to collect dust and her collection of sixty-five toe rings. Don't ask. I never have, and neither has Jean. Mama's the kind who could have a secret life as a belly dancer and pull it off without anybody ever knowing.

Mr. Grimes places his fedora on his knees while I tell him about Mama's fall and the aftermath.

"Victoria's been falling a lot lately," he says, and I feel knifed. Why didn't I know? Why didn't Jean? Good daughters would, wouldn't they?

More to the point, why didn't Mama tell us? Lord knows, she tells us everything else, even things we don't want to hear. Just last week she called for the specific purpose of lecturing me about my career. I remember her exact words.

"You're getting tunnel vision, Maggie. What you ought to do is fly to New York when Shelia gets home and see a few shows, bring some dazzle back with you."

I didn't ask Mama how she knows I'm struggling to find the words that used to flow through my soul like a sun-struck river. She never reveals her sources, but you can bet that when she speaks, she expects you to act as if you've just witnessed an oracle.

It's impossible to think of her as helpless. And falling...

Now I ask Horton, "When did Mama fall?"

"Saturday when Hattie brought her a pecan pie. She tipped over sideways on the front porch, and if Hattie hadn't caught her, she'd a landed on the wrought-iron table."

He shifts his hat on his knees. "But that wasn't the only time. She fell against her mailbox Tuesday a week ago, and before that, Hattie came running to get me when she saw Victoria crumpled in her front yard with an apronful of daffodils."

"Thank you, Mr. Grimes." Are you supposed to thank people who bring you bad news? If I were the kind of woman who cared, I'd look it up in Emily Post's book of manners.

"We're just being neighbors. You tell Victoria we'll be a-praying for her."

That's probably what Jean's doing this very minute, trying to strike up another bargain with God.

After Horton leaves, I make my bargain with Jefferson.

"If you promise to hang on to your hair until Mama's well again, I'll make us a nice chicken pot pie. How does that sound?"

If he could talk, he'd probably say, "You're going to start cooking at ten o'clock at night?"

Will Mama ever be well again? Horton's tales of falling confirm the diagnosis of a slowly fading heart.

I have to do something. Stay busy. Dance. Sing. Cook.

All three at the same time?

Why not? All that activity leaves no room for screaming.

I take out Mama's sifter and her pottery mixing dish, Mama's big wooden spoon and her glass measuring cups.

"Help me remember where these things go, Jefferson," I say, and he thumps his tail on the linoleum. "I've got to keep Mama's house exactly as she had it so that when she comes home she won't have to hunt for stuff."

The smell of chicken bubbling in good buttery crust takes me back to the day Daddy sat at the table laughing at Jean teetering around in a pair of Mama's red high-heeled shoes. I stood on the stepstool beside Mama inhaling the fragrance of chicken pie and stirring chocolate chips into batter, sneaking bites of raw cookie dough when I thought she wasn't looking.

At the age of four I thought I was fooling Mama. At the age of forty-one I know better. She was always looking, always guiding, always dreaming of the future. Not hers, but ours. Mine and Jean's.

If I scream, Jefferson will lose another patch of hair. That *was* a glob in the hallway. I checked when Horton left.

Instead of upsetting the dog, I take a blue china plate out of the cabinet and place it just so on the table, then carefully fold a linen napkin and put it on the left. Folded side in.

Or is that out?

Where is Mama when I need her? Where is my editor? My contract? My income? My future? Heck, my shoes? I kicked them off before I started dancing and now I can't remember where they are.

I'm glad I'm not the kind of woman who gets depressed and would stick her head in the oven with the chicken pie. Where would that leave poor, hairless Jefferson? And who would drive Jean home?

I switch on Mama's wall-mounted radio to see what the weather's going to be like tomorrow.

"And how are you, night owls?" Rainman asks.

"If you want to know the truth, I feel shitty," I say. I'm glad he can't hear me.

"Looks like we're in for a long haul of the wet stuff, folks. There's a front hovering over Arkansas and it's moving this way. It's a big one, too, about the size that hit Kansas and blew Dorothy's house away."

What an unusual reference for a man, but then he's from Chicago, a big radio personality who left a way of life as foreign to small-town Southerners as the back side of the moon.

"Do you have kids? And why did you leave the big city?" I ask him. Or rather, I ask the radio.

Maybe he's just somebody who likes to curl up with a children's classic on rainy days. Maybe he'd like to curl up with me—Maggie Dufrane, who is making chicken pie exactly like Mama's. Real cream and butter. No fake stuff. Love in a spoon.

"Remember the yellow brick road, folks?" Rainman continues. "Well, don't get on it tonight. You could land clear in Oz."

"If I could, I'd get on it and go clear to California, but I lost my red shoes."

Jefferson whines. "I know, but at least Rainman's company."

I wonder if he's all alone at that radio station and whether he's had dinner and if he likes chicken pot pie.

I wonder what he'd do if I called to find out.

Clearly I need…something. Something I don't have. Something I'm too tired to imagine.

After I take Jefferson out to pee and he settles onto his doggy pillow, I crawl into Mama's cedar four-poster bed and pull her white blanket under my chin.

The ringing phone jerks me upright, but when I see Stanley's number on the caller ID, I lie back down. My ex-husband's voice comes over the answering machine, amplified. "Maggie, I heard about Victoria. Call me."

I won't. We've already said everything we need to say.

Mama's blanket smells like the bath powder she uses—roses—and I snuggle there, inhaling her scent.

CHAPTER 4

It's a good morning for cuddling under the covers with your sweetie—if you're lucky enough to have one. If not and you're jockeying through traffic, keep your cool. Three minutes could be the difference between here and eternity.
—*Rainman*

I inch along behind an RV pulling a blue Honda, white-knuckling the steering wheel as I peer through the deluge.

"God, if you're listening, let that independent spirit of Mama's still be ranting and raving inside her beat-up, hooked-up body."

I circle the hospital's parking garage three times before I find a slot on the back forty. If I walk fast enough to mow down laggards, I wonder if the fifteen-minute trek to the ICU would count as exercise.

Jean is curled in a tangle of blue blankets with nothing but a few tufts of blond hair, a pert nose and the soles of her pink tennis shoes showing. She always did love to sleep with the blanket over her head. I grew up alternating between loving, sisterly hope that she wouldn't smother (eighty-five percent) and sibling-rivalry desire that she would (fifteen percent).

Now I ease into the chair beside her, wanting her to get a few more minutes rest before the hospital comes alive with anxious families filing in to console one another over the condition of loved ones.

Does Mama know she's a loved one? Did Jean and I tell her or did we take her for granted, assume she'd always be there—our safe haven in every storm?

Suddenly I've lost my appetite for sausage in Hardee's big butter-crusted biscuits, but I open the paper bag anyhow and take my first bite. Carbohydrate comfort. Greasy courage.

Jean pops out of her bunched woolly bundle. "Do I smell biscuits?" She grabs the sack and attacks her calorie-laden, fast-food breakfast.

"Has the doctor been in?" I ask.

"Not yet. They say he comes around seven." She picks fallen crumbs off her blanket and sucks them off the ends of her fingers before she starts biting her nails. "Mama's dying, Maggie."

"You don't know that."

"She never did wake up. I went in every time they allowed visitors, and she didn't respond to a single thing I said or did."

Jean's report is worse than I expected, even coming from the world's biggest pessimist.

Michael Holman is the doctor who comes in, and I feel a huge surge of hope. He's been Mama's family physician for centuries, it seems, partially because he's the only one she's never been able to intimidate but mostly because of his brilliant mind. I call him the Brain, and now I'm looking to him for miracles.

"Under the circumstances, Victoria's doing as well as can be expected."

Jean and I listen with greasy fingers linked and twin lumps in our throats.

"What, exactly, does *under the circumstances* mean?" I ask.

He reaches for my hand and I want him to hold on, want him to say *I'm here, everything's going to be all right*. Instead he says, "Hearts like hers can't survive continued trauma. All we can do now is wait and hope."

There are a million things I want to say, but I don't get a chance because suddenly he's gone, leaving me shell-shocked and lost on a chair that's minimally padded as a nod to grief. I want to call him back. I want to say, *Wait, don't go, I can't be brave alone*.

If it weren't for the courage pulsing between my fingertips and Jean's, I'd fall over. While we wait our turn to tiptoe into ICU, I hang on to my sister's hand, grateful for the resilience of women, grateful and amazed.

The silent, white-faced, shrunken-looking woman on the bed bears no resemblance to the politically active mother who stormed northeast Mississippi last summer, campaigning against the Republican candidate running for governor.

"I'd vote for a yellow dog before I'd vote for an old Republican," she said. "They're nothing but a pack of trouble."

It turns out Mama was expressing a minority opinion, but she still swears that if the Democrats had had six more people like her, they'd have won.

Make that seven and I'd say she's right.

Now Jean strokes her hair while I grab her hand and say, "Mama, you've got to wake up. We can't do without you."

I had read somewhere that hearing is the last sense to go.

Jean's standing beside the bed wadding used tissues in her fists. "She can't hear you," she whispers.

"Yes, she can. Watch this." In a voice loud enough to catch the attention of the crepe-soled, starched nurse, I say, "Mama, the governor's cut education funding again." The monitor shows changes in her vital signs, erratic lines that tell the tale of her fierce political leanings.

Jean lifts one eyebrow, still not convinced, but I keep talking to fill up the empty space, telling this shell-Mama about the camping trip she and I had planned for this summer.

"No leaky tents and crazy camp chairs for us this summer, Mama," I tell her, hoping she'll remember our trip to the Smoky Mountains right after my divorce and how we laughed at everything, even the mosquitoes that bit every movable body part and the chair that folded up when she still sat in it. According to Mama, it was obviously manufactured by Republicans.

In the sterile, too-white, too-quiet space of the curtain-enclosed cubicle, I keep fear of a Mama-deprived future at bay with talk of normal comings and goings, plans for spring cleaning and garden mulching and walks to the lake with Jefferson.

But when our time is up and we're in the hall, with Mama sealed behind heavy doors warning that visitors can come in only during allowable hours, I am bereft, even of words—especially of words.

Jean blows her nose hard and loud, not caring that grief is messy. "I want to pick out caskets," she says.

I stare at her, shocked. "That's morbid. Stop it."

"One of us has to be practical."

"For Pete's sake, Jean. Mama's not dead."

"Did you see the way she looked? Not a speck of color. Not a twitch." She honks her nose again using the same wadded, torn tissue. I fish in my purse and hand her a new one. "I'm not fixing to let her die without proper preparations."

I'm breathing hard and fast, trying to hold on to sanity. Somebody has to.

"Come on, Jean. We'll talk about this in the car."

I can't abide scenes, especially public ones. Mama once told me, "Maybe if you'd bawled Stanley out a couple of times instead of pussyfooting around, the two of you would still be together."

Maybe she was right. When I get back to the farm, I might find a spot where Mama's neurotic dog can't hear me and practice screaming. Better yet, I'll call Janice Whitten and try to un-stall my career.

Beside me, Jean is saying, "I'm not fixing to crawl into that car with you until I know where you're headed."

"Not to any funeral home, I can guarantee you that."

* * *

"Mama wouldn't be caught dead in a pink casket," is what Jean is telling the skinny, unctuous undertaker, while I hover behind her, mad at myself for ending up at Eternal Rest Funeral Home planning for Mama's demise.

By the time I backed the car out of the hospital parking space, Jean had cried enough to fill a Jacuzzi hot tub. Tears win over logic every time.

Now she asks, "What do you have that matches red? Mama wants to be buried in red."

"I didn't know that," I say. "How come I didn't know that?"

"Because you were too busy getting rid of Stanley to talk about anything else."

It's not enough that I've practically lost my sassy, cantankerous mama; I'm losing my sister, too, because I'm fixing to haul off and slap her into next Sunday. I haven't been this mad at Jean since she broke the head off my wedding Barbie. I was five years old at the time, and I shoved her into the wading pool as retaliation.

If I punch hard enough she'll land in the prissy, pink casket she blackmailed me into seeing. Fortunately, my reasonable, civilized side reasserts itself—the one who recognizes I'm enraged at congestive heart failure, not my sister; the one who curbs childish impulses and baser instincts.

Besides, it's not Jean's fault she married a saint and I married somebody who forgot to appreciate my finer qualities. I sidle up to her and reach for her hand. Grown-up. Supportive. A great big pushover.

"Let's look at the upscale line," I say.

Clinging together as if we're already orphaned, Jean and I follow the weasely-looking man into another room where the array of resting places screams ostentation. I decide on the spot to be cremated.

But, lord help me, I'll never mention the subject to Mama again. Three years ago when Stanley's grandmother died and I told Mama I thought cremation was a sensible, civilized alternative to pouring money into a six-foot hole, she said, "If Ruth Ann Dufrane is fool enough to be scattered in Lake Piomingo and end up as goose shit, that's fine with me, but I plan to go out in style. Lay me out in my good pearls and put me on display. I want a proper send-off. And you'd better not put me in a tacky, cheap casket, either."

When the undertaker pitches a sleek casket without ornamentation, I tell him, "Pricier. Mama wants to be buried in style." I point to a model that looks fit for Catherine the Great. "How about that one?"

The undertaker smiles, but Jean says, "I don't know.

The pillow looks awfully uncomfortable. Maggie, why don't you climb inside and try it out?"

Obviously grief has unhinged her. I grab a tight hold on her arm and hustle her out.

"Wait a minute," she says. "I'm not finished. What are you doing?"

"I'm getting you out of here before you come up with any other harebrained schemes—like burying me alive to see how Victoria Lucas will adjust to the dark."

On the way home, Jean makes it perfectly clear that the casket business is unfinished, and I see my future unroll as a series of daily visits with undertakers, Jean finding fault with every casket and me barely avoiding jail by not strangling her. I'll turn into a female human version of loyal Jefferson, going along with every crazy notion but sacrificing my hair.

"Somebody's got to call Aunt Mary Quana." Jean rescues me from imaginary baldness, but I'm still on my pity pot. Of course, the *somebody* she means is me.

"If I call her, she'll strike out in that old land yacht of hers and blow everybody between here and Atlanta off the road," I tell my sister.

Aunt Mary Quana has the size of a rat terrier and the heart of a pit bulldog. She views her 1969, fishtail

Cadillac with the souped-up engine as a race car and all roads as the Talladega Speedway.

I can just see the headlines: Seventy-Year-Old Woman Jailed for Doing 95 in a 40-mile Speed Zone. That, or Reckless Geriatric Claims 6 Lives in 5-Car Pileup.

"Let's wait a while before we call her," I add.

"We can't keep it a secret forever. Aunt Mary Quana will kill us."

If Mama doesn't do it first. She believes in being the center of attention. The bigger the audience, the better.

"At least let's wait till Mama's out of intensive care."

"You assume she'll get out. Alive."

"Of course, she will. Mama's too feisty to die, especially right off the bat. She likes lots of drama."

Jean punches me on the arm. "You're awful."

"I made you laugh, didn't I?"

"Yeah, but don't think you made me forget about the caskets. Because you didn't."

"I know. I *know*."

"Then we can look again tomorrow?"

"Sure."

What else do I have to do? No meals to prepare, no contract to fulfill, no heroes to seduce.

Lord, lord, how can I think about sex at a time like this? I must be depraved.

Or deprived.

As I go inside Jean's house to make sure burglars and rapists are not hiding in her closet with her forty-five pairs of shoes—mostly pink—to pillage and ravish and do no telling what-all to my helpless sister, I think about the amazing power of the mind to keep panic at bay by refocusing on the frivolous and the unnecessary. If you consider sex frivolous…and I guess it ought to be at a time like this. But wouldn't it be a great release?

Of course, casket hunting is totally unnecessary, but if it keeps Jean from breaking apart, I'm willing to do the driving.

As I drive back to Mama's, I focus on another thing, not at all frivolous. Finances. Mine. Given the current state of my bank account, I can keep a roof over my head another six months.

When I divorced Stanley, I never dreamed I'd lose my muse and my career along with my spouse. The divorce settlement was puny, to put it politely, not because Stanley's stingy and didn't want what I'm worth, but because I'm proud and didn't want to depend on him for anything.

I would live on what I earned. I would be an independent woman. I would be Mama only less...oh, I don't know...less everything. Nobody can duplicate her kind of hocus-pocus razzamatazz.

I store milk, stash dog food and then grab my checkbook on the way to the kennel. While Jefferson races around Mama's backyard debating the merits of forsythia versus hydrangea bushes, I flip open the checkbook cover and start searching for errors.

The way my lump-sum divorce settlement has dwindled, you would think I'd been flitting off to Milan for couture dresses and Pamplona to run with the bulls instead of shopping the bargain aisles of the grocery store and checking out Wal-Mart for T-shirts without slogans that declare Hot Mama or Street Angel.

Alas, I did the math right. There's no windfall in my checkbook. I'll just have to hope that when I pick up telephone messages from my apartment, my new editor has called to gush and salivate over my latest mystery.

Jefferson is relieving himself on trees now. As soon as he finishes marking his territory, I'm going straight to the telephone. I whistle for him, but my mouth is dry and this comes out as a wimpy sound that wouldn't bring anything on the run, let alone a dog determined to christen every tree along the back fence.

I hear a sharp whistle and Jefferson trots over to

have his ears scratched by my pressed, white-shirted ex-husband.

In a fit of temporary weakness, I think about trotting over myself to see if Stanley will scratch me where I itch, but I'm too embarrassed to admit it. But, oh, where would be the sizzle, the can't-get-enough-of-you, tumbling-all-over-the-bed, sweat-drenched lust? Where would be love?

"Nobody called back so I came by to find out about Victoria."

I give him a brief rundown, and when he says sorry, I know he means it because he really loves my mother.

"Is there anything I can do for you?"

"Nothing," I reply, "but thank you anyway."

He presses, trying to take charge, as usual. "She's fine, I'm fine," I assure him. "We're all fine here."

I'm in charge this time around, is what I'm really telling him, at least I'm trying to be, never-mind that I'm holding financial doom and here stands lost security.

But there's more to life. There has to be. I'm not fixing to settle for humdrum until I find out about razzle-dazzle. I'm not fixing to sit on the bench while somebody else calls the shots just because he has dangling body parts.

Ignoring the glob of hair that detaches from Jefferson's shivering coat and falls on my shoes, I slam into the house after Stanley leaves, whiz to the telephone and pick up messages. No word from my new editor. *She's read it and hates it.*

Creeping panic steals my ability to act, to pick up the phone and call Janice. In spite of closing my eyes and counting to ten, the thought keeps on coming, gathering steam, propelled by the writer's greatest fear—never being published again.

I refuse to let it beat me. Instead, I'll think of something to celebrate—life and me emerging from the safe cocoon of stultifying sameness. I go to Mama's cabinet and pull out a bottle of Gabbiano pinot grigio, 2003. Not a very good year. A married year. The year Stanley and I went to Niagara Falls for a fatal reconciliation.

Well, I'll fix that in a hurry. Two glasses and I won't even remember that after he and I finally aired our feelings, we ended up swapping our room with its hopeful king-size romping ground for one with two doubles so we could sleep in separate beds.

The second honeymoon might have worked if we wanted the same thing, but we don't. He wants a wife who folds his socks, cooks his dinner and adheres to his routine—wake at six, sleep at ten and sex every other Saturday. I want fairy-tale romance and earth-moving sex, pink-chiffon evenings and long, slow waltzes to the melted-butter voice of Andy Williams.

"Cheers," I tell Jefferson.

There are times when talking to a dog can make you feel less lonely, but this is not one of them. I switch on WTUP-FM radio, and Rainman Jones says, "There is absolutely no letup, folks. It's pouring again and the streets are not where you want to be."

Where I want to be is in my own place, a cozy cottage with a sunny front yard just right for roses and a shaded backyard big enough for a dog and a little courtyard that invites the muse. At the rate I'm going, I figure I'll be able to afford that by the year 2035.

If I live that long.

And I certainly won't if I head back to the hospital for allowable visiting hours, driving on wet streets, drunk. I pour the rest of my wine down the sink, glare at my checkbook a while, and then give it a sharp slap.

I won't cry. *I won't.*

CHAPTER 5

Looks like the rains are slacking and the clouds are beginning to break up, folks. But don't get out your sunglasses just yet, 'cause more of that nasty wet stuff is on the way.
—*Rainman*

I feel like an English muffin split in two. Half of me wants to be racing down the hospital's corridor with Jean so Mama won't be alone. Daddy was alone when his truck fell through a bridge on the county road that crosses the farm and he died in the rain-swollen river. Mama was in the kitchen making chicken potpie while Jean and I were in her bedroom flipping through movie magazines and trying to deal with raging teenage hormones. If it's within my power, I'll never let Mama face death alone.

But lord, the other half of me wants to be looking

for a job. Something temporary that will tide me over until I'm once again a working writer. I picture myself driving to my new chef's job in a white paper hat that reads Burger King.

But what are my credentials? Burger King won't care a whit about an M.A. degree in fine arts, and I can't see the likes of Woody's and Gloster 205 lining up to employ a waitress who would never keep Stanley's socks straight, let alone rib eye, medium rare, versus sirloin, medium well.

I won't think about that now. Instead I'll marshal good thoughts, positive energy I can carry into Mama's cubicle. Although none of my visions has come true in the last few months—my name splattered all over the *New York Times List* and me in the Plaza celebrating, sans clothes, with a George Clooney look-alike— I still believe in the power of the mind to manifest fabulous results.

Here's what I'm picturing: Mama awake and demanding a bath, Kentucky Fried Chicken and her daughters. In that order.

Here's what I get: Mama propped in bed in a faded gray hospital gown with a cup of chicken broth untouched on her dinner tray.

"They couldn't kill me on the operating table, so

now they're trying to starve me to death," she says, and Jean starts crying.

"Postoperative patients always get liquids," I tell her. "How long have you been awake?"

"Long enough to know I don't belong in this place. Tell the doctor to get me out of here. I haven't slept a wink with all the commotion."

"You've done nothing but sleep."

"How would you know? I've been in here by myself."

That's what I get for contradicting Mama. If it weren't for the wicked gleam in her eye, I might mistake her statement for self-pity. But that's beneath her. She's aiming for bigger impact—center stage as Drama Queen.

Jean stops crying long enough to ask Mama if there's anything she can do to help.

"Yes," Mama says. "Tell me who's called to see about me. I'm marking the ones who didn't off my Christmas-card list."

The young intern who admitted her arrives in the middle of Mama's plans for revenge. While he's checking her vital signs, she tells him she's ready to go home.

"You'll be here a while longer, Mrs. Lucas, but we're moving you to a private room."

"I don't need a private room. All I need is a few

antibiotics and some peace and quiet. Write me a prescription and send me home."

"Now, now, dearie, you're not the doctor here. I am." He pats her hand as if she's a sweet little old lady. *Major* mistake.

"I'm not senile, young man." She dismisses him with her Queen Victoria look, and turns to me and Jean. "Bring my red gown with the feathers. If Hitler is going to hold me hostage, I'm not going to stay here with my back end hanging out."

Mama's back, I'm thinking, but in the hallway outside ICU, the doctor cuts my exultation short by telling us that she's not out of the woods yet. At her age and in her condition anything could go wrong.

"Don't let her brave front fool you," he says.

"That's not a front," I tell him. "That's Mama."

If I could bottle her spunk and sell it at Piggly Wiggly, I'd be rich. I'd take her to the Swiss Alps where doctors have found a miracle cure for damaged hearts, and she'd move to a cute chalet beside a snow-capped mountain and live to be a hundred and eighty-five.

Jean stays at the hospital with her blue blanket and her cell phone, burning up the airwaves with good news to Walter, who's making my sister smile in the way of a woman talking to a man who is the center of her universe.

The only man I talk to is Jefferson, who licks my feet the minute I let him out of the kennel. Which is not too shabby, if you stop to think about it. In fact, he's the perfect man. Obedience trained. He comes when I call, sits when I tell him and never leaves the toilet seat up. Faithful and adoring. He follows me everywhere and sits at my feet salivating.

I ruffle his fur and scratch his ears. "You're nice to have around. Do you know that, old guy?"

His loose skin stretches back in a canine smile, and his pink tongue lolls out, big as a dishcloth and twice as wet.

Such is life. Some people get telephone sex and I get doggy drool.

"If Jefferson keeps losing his hair, I'll have enough to stuff a La-Z-Boy recliner," I tell Jean.

"What are you going to do about him when Mama comes home?"

"I'm thinking gorilla glue and a wig."

We're huffing up the steps to my apartment where I'll check telephone messages and grab a few clean clothes. Jean's short hair fuzzes up and her arms are full of the movie magazines she has carried to the hospital every day for the last two weeks so she can read about the marital misdoings of Tinseltown's stars while she tends Mama's needs.

My frazzled appearance is nothing compared to my frazzled nerves. Although I sit far into the night with hopeful pen and paper, nothing is happening. In my present state I couldn't write the copy on the back of a cereal box, let alone a saleable novel. If I were Virginia Woolf, I'd load my pockets with rocks, go down to the same creek that claimed Daddy and jump in.

Newton Cramer waylays us outside my door. "I saw you out here. I've been watching things for you."

One of the many advantages of living in a small Southern town is that a neighbor can watch your apartment through the peephole in his door and, for the most part, you can tell him thank you instead of calling the law.

Sometimes it's the small kindnesses that keep us going. Sometimes it's this sort of unselfish caring that makes it possible to put one foot in front of the other, to keep moving forward no matter what.

I thank him, and we go inside and sink onto my sofa. The two of us make quite a pair—middle-aged women who ought to be sitting in easy chairs with a glass of champagne in our hands and Somebody Special rubbing our feet, getting ready for an evening of succulent shrimp in real butter and lazy caresses between crisp white sheets. Instead we're exhausted from running on adrenaline, frazzled from worry and itching for somebody to blame.

"Every fifteen minutes Mama wants a drink of water," Jean says. "If I drank as much as she does, I'd pee the Pacific. Fortunately I have Walter to complain to. What you need is somebody nice, Maggie."

"Nice for you. Your husband worships you. All I got was a little lip service."

"Boy, I could use some of that. I'll be glad when Walter comes home."

"You're awful."

I punch her arm and she punches me back. This little horseplay feels good, normal, and I'm thinking that if Jean and I let this part of ourselves go, this childlike joy and abandon, we'll be letting the best part of Mama disappear.

She's never been one to sacrifice humor to mind-numbing, body-killing routine, no matter what the circumstances.

The summer ten years ago when Aunt Mary Quana watched Uncle Larry fight his last battle with Alzheimer's, we all went to Atlanta to lend moral support—Mama and Jean in the back seat nursing a cooler of fried chicken, potato salad and double-fudge-brownie pie, and me in the front seat driving. While

Jean and I cooked and cleaned and kept in telephone touch with our spouses, Mama stayed cooped up in the bedroom with Aunt Mary Quana trying to talk her through the final stages of Uncle Larry's long goodbye.

For days Jean and I heard nothing but Mama's voice and Aunt Mary Quana's sobbing. Then one morning we woke up to the sound of belly laughter. Mama was sitting in her sister's room wearing a red bulbous nose, a pink fright wig and the Mexican sombrero Uncle Larry had bought in Tijuana, just sitting there talking about the weather as if she were wearing a linen suit and pearls instead of clown garb. She wore her costume for three days, even to the Olive Garden the evening I drove her and Aunt Mary Quana out for dinner.

The next day, Mama was back in normal clothes, but she'd done what she'd set out to do—make her sister laugh and give her the boost she needed to hold Uncle Larry's hand at the end in sweet, serene farewell.

Now I turn to my sister and say, "Let's go to the movies. A comedy. Something to make us laugh."

"When Mama gets out of the hospital?"

"Yes, but before that, too. Then we can tell Mama about it, give her something to laugh about."

"Well…okay." Jean tears up and I go into the bathroom for a clean tissue. "I'm not going to cry," she says.

I don't say, *Yes, you are;* I just walk away knowing

she will, knowing that tears release her in the same way laughter does Mama.

I gather clean clothes and some gardening shoes because Mama's flower beds are getting grassy, and I want to weed before she comes home so she can enjoy her gardens. She loves flowers, loves puttering around in the dirt, making things grow. If she gets out soon we can plant roses together.

Next I go into my office to get two books—one on Native American legends because there's a strain of Cherokee blood in my veins calling to its ancestors and another titled *Soul Mates* because…

Don't ask me why. I think it has to do with the kind of unflappable optimism that lets women come back from one crushed dream after another still full of hope, their wings dragging and dusty and frazzled but intact, folded and tucked under until they grow strong enough to fly again.

The light on my answering machine is blinking. I go to the door and call to Jean, "I'm going to check messages. I'll just be a minute."

"Okay. Take your time."

I close the door, sit in my swivel chair, punch a button and hear the electronic voice of my machine. "You have six messages."

The first five are from friends checking on Mama,

three of mine and two of hers. "Congratulations," I say to the quavery recorded voices of Laura Kate Lindsey and Annie Maycomb. "You've just made Mama's A-list."

There's still no word from Janice Whitten, who obviously hates cats and doesn't know fried catfish and hush puppies from Robert E. Lee.

Okay, this is my career. With Shelia, I just picked up the phone and called. So why am I standing here as if I have no control?

I dial Janice's direct number.

"You must have read my mind," she says. "I was getting ready to call you."

She has the hint of magnolias in her voice, and when I ask her if she's Southern, she says, "I came to New York right out of Loyola. After six months in a small law firm, I realized I was in the wrong business, so I took the lowest job on the totem pole here and worked my way up."

Pecan pralines and café au lait in the French Quarter, Cajun boiled shrimp and paddle-wheelers on the Mississippi, oaks dripping with Spanish moss and harmonicas playing gut-punching blues. Janice Whitten knows them all. I promise myself I'll never make another judgment without knowing the facts first.

She tells me all the things she loved about my proposal, the richly drawn characters, the strong sense of place, even the plot.

"But this one doesn't have that special spark that made me fall in love with your early books. I'm sorry."

I see my dream cottage, my dream dog, my dream rave reviews recede into the mists. My wobbly legs won't hold me, and I sit down while Janice tells me she'll send a letter with suggestions.

"Maggie? What's wrong?"

Jean's in the doorway wearing streaked mascara and sisterly concern. I jump like somebody electrocuted.

"Don't sneak up on me like that."

"I didn't sneak. You didn't hear me, that's all."

I recap the conversation with Janice, and Jean leans her face against my hair and says, "Go ahead and cry, Maggie. It'll do you good."

"I'm not fixing to cry." I blink. Hard. And then I jump up and slap the telephone. "I just wanted her to buy the manuscript, not have sex with it."

I stomp and storm around my office, releasing shock, disbelief and fear through the soles of my feet. Writers write, don't they? They should have contracts and deadlines and readers who love them, shouldn't they?

If I'm not a writer, who am I?

I want to scream, but who would I scream at—certainly not Janice Whitten, who turned out to be a really nice person, and definitely not my sister, who's silently swiveling in my chair.

Mama would know what to say. She'd turn this tragedy into a small setback with one pithy statement.

But Jean's not Mama. She's soft and big-hearted and needy. When I run out of steam and lean my flushed face against the cool windowpane, she says, "You'll think of something, Maggie. You always do."

That was when Mama was at the helm of this family leading the cheers or cracking the bullwhip, whatever she deemed necessary. Right now, I can't think of anything except crawling back into my Jeep and driving.

At least I can do that. Shoot, as many miles as I've traveled hauling Jean and Mama, I excel at chauffeuring. I'm the world's expert, the only woman I know who can make fifteen trips a day between my apartment and Mama's farm—fourteen of them unnecessary—and still have a life. If you call birthdays alone on the fire escape and having to plan your own surprise parties a life.

We get to Jean's and she's locked out of her house, her key inside her other purse and her spare hidden in a "good place" that takes us twenty-five minutes to find. Oh, I'm on a roll here.

So why am I not surprised when I arrive at Mama's to find Jefferson shedding hair in his kennel and Mama's toilet stopped up? I shout and beg and plead at the water overflowing the toilet bowl when I flush, but it keeps on coming, soaking my shoes and Mama's favorite white cotton bath mat. I might as well pack my bags and head to Tijuana, get an oversize Mexican sombrero and live out the rest of my life herding donkeys and drinking tequila.

I race to the kitchen, grab a mop and tackle the mess while Jefferson tries to hide under Mama's bed. It's two inches from the floor and he won't fit. Thank goodness. At the rate I'm going, he'd stay there the rest of his natural life, and I'd have to spend my remaining days on my belly, hand-feeding him Fit & Trim.

"Look at it this way, Jefferson. At least I know how to use a commode plunger."

An hour later he's staring at me with his ears flattened and his fur falling while I try to think of new and creative ways to address the malfunctioning toilet. I've gone through my vocabulary of expletives. Twice. Now I've not only lost my future on this earth but one in the afterlife, as well.

Mama would disown me. Or applaud me. With her it's impossible to tell.

Remembering her quick transition from frail,

machine-dependent woman to feisty queen demanding a red-feathered gown, I attack the toilet with renewed vigor.

"I'm not giving up," I tell Jefferson.

But thirty minutes and two broken fingernails later, I do. In the way of loyal pets who understand body language and battered emotions, he sidles up to me and rubs his big head against my leg.

His canine compassion is my undoing. I slump to the floor, wrap my arms around him and fall apart.

What I need is to be somebody else, somebody with a healthy mama, a job and a twenty-year mortgage. I want to climb in bed and stay forever, creeping out only to answer the call of nature and the telephone.

Instead I get up and start dusting Mama's collectibles—not just the tops and bottoms but each tiny ceramic leg of her dogs and every miniature feather of her carved angels. They've left imprints in the dust on her whatnot shelves, and I carefully wipe that off before I set them back in the exact spot.

There's something soothing about this tedious task, something that says, *Here's an orderly woman, a woman who knows how to endure*.

Oh, lord, I never wanted mere endurance. I want triumph. Joy. Amazement.

But for now I'll take what I can get.

Next I'll change sheets on Mama's bed and clean the kitchen and vacuum the rugs and iron the curtains. Well, I'll wash them first.

But what if the washing machine's drain is connected to the toilet? Will I flood the utility room, wash the whole house into the street?

Suddenly I lose my taste for frenzied activity. I'm still hanging on to a rose quartz angel when Jefferson trots to the front door whining—and there stand Hattie and Horton Grimes with two pecan pies and every kind of salad known to man.

"We heard Victoria was a-coming home tomorrow and thought you might be needing this," Miss Hattie says.

"If there's anything else we can do, let us know," her husband adds.

When I tell him about the toilet, he says, "I've got just the thing to fix it."

Sometimes, suddenly, there's mercy. And my gratitude is immeasurable.

CHAPTER 6

There's some more May sunshine on the way, folks, so roll up your sleeves and get out in the garden. Plant a rose. Plant a tree. Leave your little patch of earth better than when you found it.
—*Rainman*

"Do you think Mama will like this?" Jean's holding a beautiful phaleanopsis orchid full of blossoms that look like white butterflies.

"She'll love it."

Mama loves everything about Mother's Day, partially because Jean and I always give her flowers, but mostly because she's the center of attention. Of course, she has to be since she's the only one in this family with offspring. Not that Jean and I ever let that stop us from celebrating. Usually the two of us doll up the Saturday before and go to a late-night spot where there's music and dancing and plenty of cheap wine. We spend the evening toasting each other and talking about how wonderful our children would have been if we'd had any.

This year, though, it's all we can do to muster energy to drag ourselves to my Jeep and make at least three trips a day to the hospital. Any less and Mama would pretend she didn't even know our names.

We find her telling Dr. Holman he ought to be ashamed of himself, keeping a fifty-five-year-old woman in the hospital so long.

"Why, Victoria, I thought you were seventy-five."

"Not when you're around," she says. Then she winks and adds, "I could give you a run for your money."

Mama's a big flirt, and today, dressed in her red gown, she looks every inch the woman who got rave reviews on Broadway and would have been a star if she hadn't followed her heart to Mississippi and settled for being the sun for her husband and the moon and stars for her daughters.

While Mama and Jean are admiring her orchid, Dr. Holman motions me into the hall. I think he's going to give me simple instructions for Mama's care after we check her out of the hospital.

Instead this man, his gentle hands and healing touch, this Brain with his reassuring ways and a pocketful of miracles tells me there will be no miracles for Victoria Lucas.

"Maggie, there's no easy way to say this. The trauma of surgery further weakened her already-failing heart."

"You're telling me Mama's dying?" *Please*, I'm thinking. *Please, no*.

"She's in no immediate danger of that, but the nature of this illness is a slow but steady decline."

"How slow?"

"At best, I'd say she has seven years. But I can't guarantee that. She's likely to experience more severe problems such as this perforated ulcer."

He takes my hand. Not a good sign. Every time Michael Holman does that it's a signal he's getting ready to deliver news I don't want to hear.

"Maggie, Victoria's going to need round-the-clock care."

Impossible, I want to shout. *Not my mama*. She's indomitable, immune to the small tragedies that befall ordinary people.

"You have to make certain she gets plenty of rest, eats properly, takes her medicine and doesn't take any chances that will result in unexpected falls."

Oh, lord. Who will do this? Certainly not my sister who falls apart at the drop of a hat.

I don't want to know the answer, don't even want

to think about it. I've only recently made my big bid for freedom and independence. How can I start moving backward?

Now Dr. Holman is saying to me, "There are many good facilities in this area that provide assisted care living. If you need my help getting Victoria into one, let me know."

Mama would die before she'd move into a nursing home. She's made her views on them perfectly clear.

Suddenly I remember a favorite saying of hers: *When the jackass is in the ditch, get it out.*

"Thank you, Dr. Holman. I'll let you know." I walk into Mama's room trying to look like a normal daughter instead of somebody trying to figure out how to get the jackass out of the ditch.

I tell Jean what the doctor said while we check Mama out. It takes two hours to get through the red tape, but finally we arrive home, and the smile on Mama's face is all the proof I need that I was right to say no to Dr. Holman's offer.

The Victoria Lucas standing in the middle of her bedroom with her hands on her hips and her lips pursed is the Mama I imagined bringing home.

Doctors can be wrong.

"What happened to my dog?"

Jefferson thumps his tail at the sound of her familiar, commanding voice, and another glob of hair plops onto the floor.

"He missed you," I tell Mama. "We all missed you."

"Flitter, you were just glad to get rid of me." She finishes her inspection of Jefferson, then goes to check out her collection of angels. She gives the pink quartz one a half-quarter turn, and then eyes Jean and me with her take-no-prisoners look. "But I'm back, and don't you forget it."

I want to put my arms around her frail shoulders and beg her not to leave us again. I want to say, *Mama, I've lost everything, I can't lose you.*

But she despises syrupy scenes, and so I say, "Hallelujah."

"Amen," Jean says.

"Quit that kidding around. I'm hungry." She sits in her recliner and pulls a red lap robe over her legs. "Jean, fix me a plate. Hattie said she brought some of that good chicken salad. But her potato salad gives me indigestion so you might as well not put it on my plate."

"Mama, chicken salad's not enough," Jean says. "You need to build up your strength."

"If you want somebody to eat it, you eat it yourself."

She dismisses Jean, who hurries off to do her bidding. "Maggie, sit down over there. I'm worried about you."

"Why, Mama?"

"Jean has a good man to love and take care of her, but you don't. I want you to have somebody really wonderful, like your daddy. Or Laura Kate's nephew."

Charlie, the geriatric who peed on the toilet seat and drooled his soup. If Mama hadn't arranged the blind date, I never would have gone out with him. Lord, that was six months ago. Which just goes to show the pitiful state of my social life.

"I'm doing fine." Small white lie. "And I'm definitely not interested in Charlie Lindsey." The gospel truth.

"Maybe I'll go out with him myself. I'm looking for a younger man."

"The one thing I know about you, Mama, is that if you wanted a man, you'd have one by now."

Shutting her eyes and leaning her head against the back of her recliner, she says, "I'm tired. I don't want to talk. Go on and let me rest." Then she sneaks a peek with one eye to see if she's fooling me.

I pretend she is. For all I know, Mama has men stashed all over Mooreville. I wonder if Jean knows. After all, she knew about Mama's preferred funeral garb. What else does she know that she's not telling me?

I tiptoe to the kitchen, just in case Mama's not playing possum. Jean is standing at the sink, wearing Mama's faded, flower-sprigged apron, her shoes kicked off and one bare foot resting on top of the other one as she arranges chicken salad on freshly washed lettuce leaves.

"How is she?" my sister asks.

"I honestly don't know."

When she tears up, I say, "Don't you dare let her see you cry. We have to try, here, Jean. We all have to try."

"I know. I'm just thinking about what the doctor said."

I am, too, but tears won't help.

The Victoria Lucas I brought home is *not* the woman I expected. Mama is shedding her invincibility bit by bit—swollen legs here, birdlike appetite there, flying-off weight everywhere. She's leaving us slowly, not going softly into the night but blazing through our universe with the brilliance of a comet burning itself out.

Her new walker, standing in the hallway, is mute evidence.

CHAPTER 7

It's another sunny day in May, but it looks like some rough weather ahead. There's a storm front pounding the Gulf Coast and it's headed this way. Batten the hatches. We're in for a gully washer.
—*Rainman*

Storm clouds gathering on the southern horizon mirror exactly how I feel, my insides boiling with tumult and indecision. No wonder Mama's worried about me. I'm a woman coming undone with nothing left to hold me together except dogged determination.

Daddy used to go for a walk every time he had something heavy on his mind, and today that's what I'm doing, walking with Jefferson while Mama naps. Squatting beside a stream, I pick up a handful of soil and let it sift between my fingers. This will endure—fertile earth and winding waters, spreading oaks and soft green grasses that cushion my footfall.

Like Carter Lucas, I've always taken comfort and courage from the farm. He used to tell me, "No matter what happens to us, Maggie, this land will go on."

Together we would sit in the shade of an ancient oak and read Native American wisdom. One of my favorite sayings was from Seattle, chief of the Suquamish tribe: "All things are connected. Whatever befalls the earth befalls the children of the earth."

Now I plop down on the root of an ancient black walnut tree, close my eyes and listen to the earth breathe, simply listen. It's a peaceful, steady sound, one that makes you want to fall into it and float.

Jefferson puts his head in my lap and whines.

"I know, boy. Coming home again might not be such a bad thing." Forget that I would be giving up my own place, relinquishing the little cocoon where I was going to hole up, caterpillarlike, until I could emerge with wings.

Considering my current state of affairs, the cocoon is not working. Maybe a change is in order.

Still, I want to talk with my sister. Maybe she can come up with another solution.

I dust off my slacks and walk across the pasture to Jean's. Not that I want to do anything behind Mama's back. What I don't want is Victoria Lucas saying, "Just go on home. I can take care of myself."

My sister's house sprawls all over the hilltop. She and Walter love to entertain, and built a mansion that rivals Tara in *Gone with the Wind*. Jean is in her kitchen cooking enough to feed a third-world country. Simmering pots fill every eye on her stovetop, and her oven groans with casseroles.

"I thought I'd make a few things Mama likes to eat. You can come back this afternoon and pick it up."

"Well…good," I tell her.

She's just wrecked my diet. I can't stand to waste food. I picture myself in Mama's kitchen at midnight scarfing down leftover roast beef and garlic mashed potatoes and baked ham and German chocolate cake. Emptying the dishes so I can take them back to Jean.

"Here…" Jean slices off two big slabs of cake and pours two cups of coffee. "Let's eat while we talk."

We dig in, and Jean delivers the first good news I've heard since April. "Walter's coming home this evening."

To help do some of the driving, I hope. This respite means I'll have at least a few hours to go back to my apartment and turn on my computer. Writing is a different story, though. I'm still torn between the urge to put words on a page and the fear that my muse won't be there to turn them into magic.

"That's great," I tell Jean. "How long before his next trip?" Six months is what I'm hoping for, long enough for me to grab hold of my endangered career and pull it to safety before it plunges to the bottom of the ravine.

"Three days," she says, and I hear a *kerplunk* as my unattended career hits the bottom. "That's why I'm doing all this cooking today. When Walter gets home, I don't plan to spend a single minute in the kitchen. I plan to—"

"I get the picture, Jean. Spare me the prurient details."

"You don't mind taking care of Mama while Walter's here? I mean, after all, I've hardly seen him, and he's fixing to turn right around and head off to the Philippines."

"I understand."

"Well, you don't act like it."

"What do you want me to do, Jean? Jump up and down singing 'Hot Time in the Old Town Tonight'?"

"You're still mad at me about the caskets."

"I am *not* mad at you about the caskets. Or the sex, either."

"I didn't mention sex. Did I mention sex?"

"For Pete's sake, Jean…" I'm so frustrated, I cut myself another big slice of cake. It will be all my sister's fault if I get as big as a house. "Let's just stick to the subject. What are we going to do about Mama?"

"Walter and I could hire a sitter, but she'd have a hissy fit."

Mama's already aired her views on the subject of sitters. Last year when the Maycomb brothers hired Miss Nell Plunkett to take care of their mother after she fell and broke her leg in two places, Mama said, "Poor old Annie's sitting down there depending on strangers to take her to the bathroom. When I get to the point that I can't take care of myself, just take me out to the back pasture and shoot me."

"I know she would, Jean. There's only one thing to do." I eat a large bite of cake before continuing. "I'm moving in with Mama."

"Maggie, are you sure? I know how much that little apartment means to you." This is a weak protest. Jean's mind is obviously on taking care of her house, her husband and her red-hot libido.

"Is anybody ever sure of anything?"

Considering that I no longer have the means to pay my rent—and we won't even talk about taking care of my libido—I could view my move as a blessing in disguise. But that takes more philosophical acceptance than I can muster right now. What I'm going to do is drive to my apartment and kick furniture.

But first I have to put a spin on this proposal for Queen Victoria.

On the way to Mama's I decide to present the idea as if she'll be doing me a huge favor. I'll *ask* if I can live with her a while. If necessary, I'll beg.

Mama doesn't give me a chance to do any of those things. She's in the kitchen teetering on top of a straight-backed chair, defying death and the laws of gravity.

"Good lord, Mama. What are you doing? Get down from there."

A can of creamed corn tumbles from the cabinet and rolls across the floor. Mama looks over her shoulder and scowls at me. Her intimidating look. I know it well. What she doesn't know is that it stopped working with me when I was fifteen. Well, maybe thirty-five, but that's too embarrassing to admit.

"You scared me to death," she says. "What do you mean sneaking up on me like that? You could make me fall and break my neck."

"*Exactly*, Mama." I take her arm to help her down, but she shakes me off.

"I'm not finished up here, yet."

"What do you want? I'll get it."

"You don't know where it is." She rumbles around in the cabinet, sending canned vegetables flying. I narrowly miss being beheaded.

"For Pete's sake, if you don't get off that chair I'm going to call the fire department."

"You and which army?"

Mama's trying to keep up her spitfire act, but I can tell she's tiring. I don't know how she mustered the energy to get up there in the first place. Sheer determination, I guess. Spit-in-your-face will. Piss-and-vinegar spirit. I wish I had half of that.

And maybe I do. Maybe it's the Victoria Lucas in me that says, *Yes, you can survive this change, too.*

Finally she allows me to help her down, and then leans heavily against my arm as I take her back to her recliner. When I cover her legs with the red lap robe, I notice her swollen feet and put the leg rest up.

"Where's your walker, Mama?"

"I don't need that old thing."

"Dr. Holman said you did."

"Flitter, what does he know? Miserable as a sore-tail cat and won't do a darned thing about it."

"How do you know that, Mama?"

"I have my ways."

She shuts her eyes, which means (a) she's dismissed me, and (b) whatever she was looking for wasn't important. Or else, she's forgotten. Horrible thought—Mama without the razor-sharp mind that knows every move Jean and I make.

In three seconds, Mama's snoring, but I'm afraid to leave her alone, even the few minutes it takes to go to the back yard with Jefferson. There's no telling what she will do next.

"Hurry," I tell him, and he does. He's lived with Mama so long he's almost human.

She's still asleep when I get back. If I had my computer and my files, I'd sit down, put my hands on the keyboard and see if my muses have all packed their suntan lotion and gone to Miami.

Instead I stay busy doing laundry, but the house feels lonesome—the way it felt the year Jean first went to college and Mama decided to take a job.

I was sixteen and thrilled at the prospect of having the house all to myself. While Mama terrorized the rabbit-toothed owner of the weekly newspaper who had hired her to organize his files and didn't know how to prevent her from trying to organize his life, I wandered around the empty house trying to stretch thirty-minute chores into two hours. I called my friends every fifteen minutes, but that couldn't fill the gap left by Jean and Mama, and so I took up hobbies, even ones I didn't like. Crocheting and knitting. The results are buried in the backyard, but Mama was too quick for me when I attempted to say last rites over the paintings I did with a beginner's set of acrylics. My *Four Seasons*, which all look suspiciously like spring, are still hanging in her dining room.

After six weeks, Mama pronounced her boss and his files hopeless, and came back home to take charge.

I won't think about whether she can ever take charge again. Instead, I turn on the radio for company, then stretch her gown over the ironing board and start pressing just the way she likes, bottom to top, no reversing.

I was with her when she bought this gown, bright blue with a lace-inset, pin-tucked bodice. "It'll be a good hospital gown, for when I get old," she said.

"Mama, you will never grow old," I replied.

"You've got that right," she said and, to prove her point, she dragged me to the shoe department and bought the highest pair of heels she could find, red shoes, dangerous-looking, the kind that said, *Watch out, here I come*.

"These shoes will make you change your whole attitude," she told me. "You ought to buy some."

I never did, partially because Stanley thought shoes of that sort were ridiculous, but mainly because a woman constantly behind the wheel needs sensible shoes.

Now, I wish I had. I'd put them on and wait to become a changed woman, somebody scintillating and just a bit wild, somebody who would walk onto the front porch and spit in the eye of the storm Rainman says is heading this way.

"I'll bet you like a woman in sexy shoes," I tell him. I don't know why I believe that. Something about his voice. It's deep and growly, intimate-sounding. I'd like to hear Rainman read Walt Whitman.

"Help!" Mama's cry shatters my poetic interlude and I race to her bedroom expecting to apply mouth-to-mouth resuscitation.

She's sitting up in her recliner, trying to lower the footrest, rigid with rage.

"What in the world did you put this thing up for? I can't get it down, and I'm about to die of thirst."

I help her get out of the chair, appalled at this new sign of her physical weakness. *It's temporary,* I tell myself. *Just till she builds her strength back.*

She goes into the kitchen, using her walker this time, and while she sits at the table waiting for the glass of iced water with lemon, she says, "You ought to move in with me, Maggie. I've got a perfectly good place to stay and it's paid for.

"Besides," Mama adds, "I might enjoy having a roommate."

Her instincts are amazing. Trust her to divine the problem before it's ever mentioned. There's a delicate balance here between pride and need, both Mama's and mine. I slice the lemon into perfect, careful wedges while I frame an answer that will save both our faces and prevent this powder-keg topic from exploding.

"We'll give it a try," I finally tell her, and she drinks her water, satisfied.

With one simple gesture, she turned an agonizing decision into a moment of simple hospitality and pure grace. There's an art to this. If I'm lucky and the gods of spirits-that-can't-be-broken smile on me, I'll have enough time with Mama to learn.

Moving is never easy, particularly when you're doing it during a thunderstorm. The date seemed sensible when I started out: another month's rent will be due next week and Walter, with his strong back and maroon Dodge minivan, will be gone.

The first thing I see when I get to my apartment is a letter sticking out of my box, New York postmark. I can't bear to look, can't bear the thought of dealing with a sinking career while I'm in the midst of giving up my freedom.

I stick the letter in my back pocket, then go through my apartment making split-second decisions about what to take and what to box for storage. Walter's packing my office, a must-take, while I pack personal belongings into boxes labeled Salvation Army and Mama's House. Most of the clothing that shrank two sizes just to spite me goes into the first box, but the favorites I can't bear to part with go into the second. You never know. Cindy Crawford might return the body she stole from me, and I'll be able to fit into them again.

"I've got your computer and files ready to go, Maggie. Why don't we take a little break?" Walter is sweet-faced and endearing, his jogging shoes and pant legs soaked from the rain, his faded blue T-shirt stretching across his belly in a way that says he takes too many meals at fast-food restaurants and never has time to walk on the farm he loves.

I make tea, and while we sit on the sofa I've already covered with a sheet for the movers, he thanks me for looking after Jean. And then, with a sincerity that precludes embarrassment, he says, "I know a lot of people who would hire a smart woman like you. If you need my help in that department, let me know."

"Thanks, Walter, but I can't give up on a ten-year career. Not yet."

"Good for you. In the meantime, if you need a little extra cash, all you have to do is tell me how much."

It takes a while before I can reply and he sits quietly, knowing why. Lucas pride. A never-give-up attitude. A woman determined to reinvent herself, and do it on her own terms.

"I'm fine, thank you," I finally say.

"It was nothing," he says, and I blink hard, twice. It was family and friend and mercy. It was everything.

That evening, with my belongings crowded among seventy-five years of Mama's collected memorabilia, I lie in the bedroom of my childhood listening to the sounds of her sleep, snores interspersed with occasional restless moans and mumbling.

Is she dreaming of dancing in her madcap red shoes or is she talking with Saint Peter, making bargains to be transported from this life to the hereafter in splendor and glory? I imagine myself going with her, caught up in the excitement of another grand adventure with Mama, following closely behind so I can fly on her tailwinds. Maggie, the daughter who didn't get left behind.

My forehead dampened by sweat, I snap on the lamp and, in the soft glow of the rose-colored shade, rummage in a cardboard box filled with my books. *Leaves of Grass* is a slim volume, leather-bound and beautiful, a birthday gift from Stanley fifteen years ago, back when we still had poetry between us.

"Song of Myself" is marked, and I read aloud.

"All goes onward and outward, nothing collapses, And to die is different from what any one supposed, and luckier."

Reading Whitman's words again, letting the word *luckier* melt on my tongue like strawberry ice cream, I savor the taste of hope.

And with it comes the first stirrings of my muse. I rummage in the bedside table, pull out Janice's letter and read. It's a clear and fresh look at my proposal, suggestions for changes, an affirmation, really.

Excited now, the words spilling through my mind like a waterfall, I open my laptop and start to type.

CHAPTER 8

A big hello from the folks at WTUP-FM! We're broadcasting from the courthouse square in beautiful downtown Tup-elooo! The Hog Roasters are here cooking up barbecue and Father's Day sales are going on all over town. So come on down and join us.

—*Rainman*

Rainman is singing "June is Bustin' Out All Over" and Mama and I are warbling along with him while I drive to Wal-Mart, my Brillo pad hair caught in a ponytail, my slacks getting a little baggy from long walks on the farm with Jefferson, and my spirits high. Something about the farm is settling inside me, filling up the empty spaces. Or maybe it's Mama with her big spirit and lively ways.

Though I always insist she use the walker to ward

off falls, she uses it as a stage prop rather than something to lean on. I'm hoping that when we see Dr. Holman again he'll tell us he made a huge mistake. If he had a heart like Victoria's, he'd live to be a hundred and two.

She's getting stronger every day. The only thing that concerns me is her weight: in spite of Jean's butter-laden casseroles, it continues to peel off, muscle and sinew vanishing underneath sagging skin to reveal sharp, brave bones.

We've set out to buy her some new clothes. "A temporary wardrobe," she said, "until I get my Marilyn Monroe figure back." I wanted to go downtown for a better selection, but she insisted on Wal-Mart. When I asked why, she said, "One-stop shopping. You get toilet paper, I'll get underwear that won't fall off."

I park next to the double glass doors and, while I get her walker from the back seat, she hops out of the Jeep, feisty and raring to shop.

"For Pete's sake, Mama, act decrepit. We'll get arrested for lying about this disabled sticker."

"You act old." She slings her purse over her shoulder. "You might as well put that old thing back in the car. I'm not using it."

"You have to."

"I don't have to do a thing I don't want to. I'm seventy-five years old."

"Then why did you tell Dr. Holman you're fifty?"

"None of your business." Mama prances off, and while I'm hurrying to catch up, calling her to wait, she says, "I'm going to get a motorized cart. I can get around faster that way."

Any faster and she'd be setting Olympic records for geriatrics.

Getting her an electronic cart is one thing; teaching her to drive is another. She puts it in reverse and mows down a rack of Hershey's bars and an arm-waving, red-faced clerk. She barely misses plowing through the glass doors and into the parking lot before she can stop.

"I thought you were going clear to Alabama before I could stop you, Mama."

"You tend to your business and let me tend to mine." Mama puts the cart in forward gear and roars off, scattering shoppers and scaring little children with her daredevil ways and reckless driving.

I can't look. Veering in the opposite direction, I end up staring at the covers of mass-market and trade paperback books, none of them mine. This makes me feel unwanted, untalented and unappreciated. In a word, *awful*.

Is the work I'm doing now any good? Can I really make a comeback? Or am I simply fooling myself into believing I can write with wings?

I race toward housewares, where I stand squeezing a twelve-pack of Angel Soft. Mama whizzes up in her cart and says, "What are you doing, just standing there? Grab that toilet paper and come on."

"Where are you going?" She zips past me and around the corner. "Mama, come back here. I'm talking to you."

People turn to give me funny looks because clearly I'm talking to myself. I try to catch up with Mama without running. No small feat.

The gods of mother-daughter disputes are with me. When I round the corner, I see her stalled in the shoe department, rocking the cart back and forth as she jerks the gears from forward to reverse.

"Mama, what are you doing?"

"I can't get this farty old thing to move."

I lean over to check the gears, but the cart sits there spinning while she fumes. "Turn it off, Mama. I'm going to check it out."

Well…here I am on all fours in the middle of Wal-Mart, hoping nobody notices my butt the size of a Texas spread.

There's a big, fuzzy, purple house shoe stuck under

the back left wheel, and I give it a tug, expecting it to pop right out. But no. When Mama does a thing, she goes whole hog.

I groan upward and tell her the good/bad news. "I'm going to have to tilt the cart a little," I tell her.

"I'll get out and help."

"You will *not*." With Herculean effort, I heave the back of the cart upward. While Mama teeters in the air—enjoying herself because she's the center of another big drama—I kick at the house shoe. It takes three tries before I dislodge it and free the wheel. My back protests as I lower the cart.

"Wonder Woman to the rescue," I say. "Let's get some Ben-Gay and go home. I need to turn in my cape."

"I don't think she wore one." Mama peels off for the pharmacy while I creak and lurch along in her wake. When I arrive, she's holding the back-rub ointment and announcing to everybody within hearing distance, "This is my daughter, the writer. She's taking me downtown to get some barbecue."

Here's the thing about small Southern towns: it's common—and even considered polite—to strike up conversations with perfect strangers in the aisles of Wal-Mart and JCPenney and around the washbasins of public restrooms.

Here's the other thing: if you're a writer, people automatically think you're rich and famous. And they're disappointed if you're not glamorous, too.

I feel like a fraud standing there with untamed hair caught back in a rubber band and a big glob on the knee of my pants that looks suspiciously like chewing gum. Still I nod and try to act the part—I'm not Mama's daughter for nothing. If I knew the beauty-queen wave, I'd do that, too.

Satisfied, Mama puts her cart in forward gear and finally heads toward the cashier's stand.

Will this day never end? When we get back into the Jeep, Rainman is still singing, but I don't. I don't even try to talk Mama out of barbecue. If she feels like eating, I'll crawl to get her some food.

While she's napping—or leaning back thinking up more devilment—I drive along wishing I had my name on the cover of a current book and my hair pulled back with a pink bow. Something feminine and hopeful.

By the time I park in front of the courthouse, Mama's revived and ready to go while I feel as if I've been hit by a Green Bay linebacker.

And not in a nice way.

The next time I take Mama to see Dr. Holman, I'm going to ask him to put me on the same vitamin he prescribed for her.

A huge crowd mills around the hundred-year-old courthouse and the tables that have been set up near the fountain. The delicious aroma of pork roasting slowly on spits perks me up, and I get in line for two plates while Mama waits under the shade of a magnolia tree in a green-striped lawn chair one of the city's councilmen—Blake Tanner—gave up for her.

By the time I return, she's holding court with Tanner and his pretty wife, Marilyn, as well as Mayor Gibbs and his wife, Patty. In addition, she's waving toward one of the WTUP staffers who's interviewing the crowd.

"Over here," Mama says, and a tall man with beautiful hands—no ring—and a microphone heads our way.

"Well, folks…" he says. I'd know that voice anywhere. *Rainman.* "Here's one of Tupelo's stately senior citizens, enjoying the best barbecue in the South. Let's see what she has to say."

He's heading our way, and oh lord, St. Peter and all his angels…if I had dreamed him up I couldn't have found a more perfect man. Not handsome in a pretty-boy sort of way, not even the rugged, outdoor type, but something in between, some amazing combination of square jaw and cleft chin, of well-defined cheekbones and sculpted lips that piques my interest. *More* than stirs my interest. *Lord*, I'm stirred in ways I haven't felt for years.

How embarrassing is that? Here I am looking like something left over from a Hell's Angels rally when I want to look spectacular. For once in my life, I want to be the kind of woman with tanned legs that reach from here to Texas and a certain flair that makes a man fall down and worship at her feet.

I'm in trouble here.

"This is my daughter, Maggie," Mama says. "She's a writer."

I want to shrink to the size of a silver sewing needle. Instead I smile and step behind Mama's chair to hide the chewing gum on my knee. Rainman stares straight at me while self-conscious sweat trickles down the side of my face and threatens to drip off my chin.

Finally, being a consummate professional, he turns back to Mama. The man knows a talk-show gold mine when he finds one.

Kneeling in front of her chair, he leads her through a story about Tupelo being the first city in the U.S. to buy power from the Tennessee Valley Authority. Naturally she's the star of this tale because she was the only child who got a picture made with President Franklin Roosevelt when he traveled here by train in 1933 to applaud our progress.

After she's finished her story, Rainman maneuvers around her chair to stand beside me, sticky hair, gummed-up pants and all.

"Hi, Maggie. I'm Joe." His slightly crooked smile is enormously appealing. "What's your story?"

"Off the record?" I say, and he switches off his microphone. "I'm this glamorous mystery novelist who knows how to overcome a man six ways—all of them lethal."

Goodness, I'm actually flirting—something I haven't done since I can't remember when.

"I'd like to buy you a cup of coffee and explore that," he says.

In these pants? With this hair? This life? And after that come-on reply I wish I could take back? *Oh*, I think not.

"Thank you, but no. Mama's getting tired. I have to take her home."

Why didn't I say I'll take a raincheck? Here's the first man I've been interested in since Stanley and I've dismissed him.

Pressing a card into my hand, he says, "Call me when you're free," and suddenly there's hope.

He moves on and so do we. Not quickly because Mama has finally played herself out—but triumphantly, which is even better.

"You know what we ought to do, Maggie? Get ourselves a red convertible so we can drive around and people can see us."

I picture us in that sassy car, radio blaring, fancy hubcaps spinning and our hair blowing in the wind.

"Carter and I saw one on our honeymoon. It looked like Marilyn Monroe was driving, this red scarf tied around her hair and her lips painted to match like she owned the world. I wanted one so bad. Carter was going to get me one when he retired…. God rest his soul."

I could drive anywhere in a dream car like that. With me at the wheel and Mama in the passenger's seat, we could sprout wings and fly clear up to the stars.

At nine-thirty Mama finally settles in for the evening, and I call Jean to recount the day as proof she's going to outlive us all, anecdotal evidence that we are right and the doctors are wrong.

I tell Jean everything about our day except the part about meeting Rainman. This I keep to myself. I want to savor it, say his name aloud and roll it around on my tongue like some delicious secret.

I actually do this, say, "Rainman" slow and dreamlike, a fully grown woman taken leave of her senses.

Then, with my muses whispering in my ear, I sit in

front of my computer at the dining-room table and tap away at fictional mystery and mayhem, oblivious to my surroundings and the passing of time.

It's three o'clock when I finally go to bed, and the smell of perking coffee wakes me at five. Stumbling into the kitchen in my nightshirt, I see Mama with her head on the table, snoring.

"Mama, what's wrong?"

She lifts her head, rubs her eyes. "My beauty-shop appointment's at eight."

"For Pete's sake. Do you know what time it is?"

"Of course, I do. I need time to fix up. I'm not about to go to the Beauty Box looking like Ned in the First Reader."

Maybe this is a good thing. Words are flying around my head like trapped butterflies, waiting to be set free. I throw on slacks and T-shirt, then open my computer and start typing.

At seven-thirty Mama announces, "It's time to go." Although the Beauty Box is only five minutes away, I head out anyway, not out of duty but with a grateful heart that I can do one more small thing that will make my mama happy.

I pack my laptop and then tune out the roar of hair driers and the latest gossip as I dance with my muse.

* * *

There's a ritual I always perform after I've finished a writing project. It requires white candles and a full moon, a thankful heart and a wide-open mind.

Having Jean makes it better so I call her and say, "I've finished the new proposal."

"Already? Wow, Maggie. Just *wow*."

I tell her about staying up late and then taking my laptop to the Beauty Box. Then I say, "I've just typed the last sentence. Join me for the ceremony? I'll drive over and get you."

"Let me put on my robe."

This is one of the things I love most about my sister. If I'll pick her up she's always ready to go, even if it's past nine and she has already settled for the evening in front of the TV.

Mama's asleep, so I tiptoe around the house gathering white candles. They're everywhere, on tiny mirrors in her bathroom, in pink china holders on her dressing table, in cranberry glass cups along the side of her tub. I put these in a plastic shopping bag along with three chapters and a synopsis, newly conceived and freshly printed.

"Watch Mama," I whisper to Jefferson, although judging by the way she's snoring, I don't expect her to wake until the morning.

I drive to Jean's in the light of a perfect gibbous moon, not quite full, but giving that appearance. Only the discerning eye can see the slightly bulging configuration on one side of this incandescent silver orb. Only a woman who waits under Venus and knows she's standing on stardust can connect to this incredible, magical lunar queen.

Jean's watching for me, and by the time I come to a stop, she's opening the door and climbing into the Jeep. Less than ten minutes after I left, I'm back at Mama's lighting candles on her front porch.

Then Jean and I kick off our shoes, shed our robes and dance with our feet in the splendid summer grass, our white gowns twirling in the moonlight.

"Think positive," I say. "Are you thinking good thoughts, Jean?"

"I'm thinking about Walter." She says this as if she's dreaming and doesn't want to be awakened. I don't remind her, she's supposed to be sending gracious thought-prayers skyward.

Under a moon like this, it's possible to forget everything except the gardenia-laden sweetness of a Southern summer night and the heart-moon connection that makes it impossible to tell where flesh and bone end and the heavens begin. I spread my arms, embracing the world, dancing, flying.

"What are you trying to do?" Mama's voice halts me midflight. "Sneak off and have all the fun without me?" She's standing on the front porch with her walker, the white nylon nightcap she uses to protect her freshly done, beauty-salon hairdo gleaming in the candlelight. "Jean, come up here and help me down the steps."

"Mama, stay there," I tell her. "We'll join you on the porch."

"Flitter, if I'm going to dance, I've got to do it right."

Practical, earthbound daughters would lead her into the house and put her back to bed so she could get some rest, but my sister and I understand that Mama has other, more compelling needs. Fun. Laughter. Spit-in-the-eye-of-fate-and-damn-the-consequences freedom.

It takes both of us to get Mama and her walker down the front steps, and then she kicks off her shoes and hulas around the yard, her nightcap askew, her walker serving as a third silvery leg.

Somewhere above us, God is smiling.

CHAPTER 9

For those of you who haven't already been outside to see for yourself, it's a scorcher today.
—*Rainman*

Sweat is rolling down my face in spite of the Jeep's
air conditioner and my T-shirt is sticking to my skin
in wet patches that might be sexy if the rest of me
didn't look and feel so wilted. Since when did I think
I could work till three o'clock one night, dance and
party till midnight the next and get up feeling sixteen?

"Wear a hat," Rainman tells me. Well, he tells everybody in his vast WTUP audience, but I'll bet I'm
the only listener who's talking back. This would alarm
me if I didn't know better. Sensitive, artistic souls often
carry on conversations with inanimate objects and
out-of-sight people—the can opener that won't work,

the toilet that refuses to cooperate, the computer that has a mind of its own, the weatherman on the radio.

"Be Victorian," he says. "Carry an umbrella."

"Not many people know that," I tell him. "Do you read a lot?"

"The temperature is hovering around ninety and climbing," he says.

The trouble with talking to people who aren't there is that it's a one-sided conversation. And lonely, if you stop to think about it. It screams here's a woman with sweat circles under her arms, a too-tight waistband pinching her middle and newly discovered wrinkles around her eyes with nobody to complain to, a woman with unappreciated pot roast and lacy underwear collecting dust. A woman who could go on a crying jag any minute if she didn't have so much to do.

Federal Express comes into view, shimmering and ephemeral in the heat that rises in blinding white waves off the cracked pavement. I park by the front door and go inside where I address an envelope to my new editor, overnight, 10:00 a.m. delivery. I won't think *last chance* as I drop my proposal inside and seal the package. I won't think *what if*. Instead I'll remember myself dancing under the light of a gibbous moon and capturing its magic in my soul.

* * *

Before I head home, I perform ritual number two: celebrate with small indulgences. These usually come in the form of chocolate or butter and sugar. I wheel into Dunkin' Donuts determined to order only one. That way I can feel virtuous and rewarded. Any more and I descend into a sugar overdose that makes me feel sluggish and guilty.

A waitress with powdered sugar on the front of her apron comes to take my order.

"A cream-filled doughnut. Just one."

"How can you do that?" The voice behind me is deep and male. "I don't have that much willpower."

Rainman. My skin tingles and when I turn around I'm afraid he'll guess that he's the cause of my flushed face.

"Hi, Maggie." He smiles. "Do you have time for that cup of coffee?"

I have a dozen errands to do, and Mama's back home waiting, but, oh, so am I. Something inside me has been waiting for a very long time, waiting to come alive.

"Yes," I say, and join him at a small red vinyl booth, both of us with cream-filled doughnuts and steaming cups of coffee.

"I just heard you on the radio," I tell him.

"Recorded."

"I was fascinated by your reference to Victorian customs."

"I read a lot. In fact, I just finished reading one of your books, *The Cat's Meow*."

When a stranger likes you enough to hunt for a back copy, it's always gratifying. But when the stranger is Rainman, it's thrilling. He has just said to me, I like you enough to want to discover more about you.

"Thank you," I tell him, and I hope my smile says, *I'm glad you did*.

"I enjoyed it. Your heroine has a wonderful sense of humor, and I suspect, so do you."

Call me and find out, I want to say, but that only happens in fiction, so instead I tell him about the fine line writers draw between fantasy and reality, and how sometimes even we have a hard time telling them apart.

I sound like a teacher or a workshop coordinator. What do women my age talk about when they want to make a man sit up and take notice?

"That's fascinating," he says. "I'd love to hear more, but I've got to get back to the station."

He dumps our wadded-up napkins and, as we both head toward the door with our take-out coffee cups, I feel eighteen and eighty-five all at the same time, the racing pulse of a teenager and the antiquated dating skills of an octogenarian.

Not that this is a date. Still…

His car is on one side of the lot and mine on the other. We're about to go our separate ways when he turns back.

"Maggie, I never did get your number. Do you mind?"

"Of course not."

After he leaves, I have to sit a while with the air conditioner on high to cool off my hot face. Not to mention my other hot parts. *Oh, lord…*

Jean and Mama are waiting for me in my sister's kitchen with twin conspiratorial grins and fried chicken. I nab a leg from the platter as I pass by the serving bar.

"You didn't have to cook," I tell Jean, knowing she won't pay me the least bit of attention. I wouldn't pay me any attention, either, if I knew my way around a chicken the way she does. Fried, baked, roasted, stuffed, grilled—you name it my sister does it to perfection.

"I thought we would eat first," Jean tells me.

"Before what?" I say, thinking she means before I take Mama home for her afternoon nap.

"We have a little surprise." Mama's already sitting at the head of Jean's table, where she presides over all family gatherings, drinking a big glass of iced sweet tea.

Six years ago when she announced she was tired of cooking and we'd be gathering at Jean and Walter's house for Thanksgiving, Christmas, Fourth of July and birthdays, my sister and I mourned the passing of an era.

"Things won't be the same," Jean told me.

"It's not like Mama to step aside," I said.

Little did we know. Mama didn't step aside; she just changed venues.

Now Jean fixes Mama's plate, pours two more glasses of tea and joins us at the table.

"We're having a fancy dinner party," Mama says, and I don't have to see her big grin to know how much she's looking forward to the occasion. She'll wear silver shoes and sequins, no matter if it's just for family or if we've invited the Bushes, both senior and junior. Of course, we'd do that over Mama's dead Democratic body.

"Is Walter coming home?" I ask Jean.

"No, but Aunt Mary Quana is going to be here.

And Stanley because he adores her, and we knew you wouldn't mind."

"Of course not. We're friends."

"Horton and Hattie are coming," Mama says, "and Laura Kate because she went to school with Mary Quana. She's bringing her nephew Charlie."

My appetite for chicken vanishes, even if it is Jean's and it's buttermilk-crusted and deep fried.

"I can't believe you called him."

A woman who has to depend on her mother to fix her up is usually unattractive, undesirable and untouched. Well, I am if you don't count latex. Of course, I don't care what Charlie thinks, so why am I getting so worked up?

"We didn't invite him," Jean says. "Laura Kate asked if she could bring him along and we didn't want to be impolite and say no."

"Besides," Mama adds. "Somebody has to take the bull by the horns."

"Charlie's more an out-to-pasture gelding than a bull."

"Listen, Maggie, before you get all bowed up at Mama and me, just think of this party as a nice surprise for Aunt Mary Quana. Besides, you don't have to go to bed with him. Even if you are neglecting your **sex** drive."

"I can't believe you said that in front of Mama."

"How do you think you got here?" Mama says. "Immaculate conception?"

I flounce off to Jean's family room to get away from meddlers. But not without my plate of chicken. I can't fight back if I waste away to a swizzle stick.

Long after I've taken Mama home, I stew about the problem, tossing and turning and watching the hands on the bedside clock. I've just dozed off when I hear noises in Mama's bedroom. Racing in, I discover her hair drenched and her gown glued to her body.

"I'm calling Dr. Holman."

"Maggie, no. It's night sweats. Heartburn. I ate too much at Jean's. Help me change these sheets."

"Sit down, Mama. I'll do it. But first I'm going to get you out of that wet gown and check your blood pressure."

Not that I'm any good at nursing. The cuff inflates automatically and the numbers print out digitally— 110/60. A bit low, but nothing alarming, especially for Mama. I won't panic and pick up Jean for a midnight run to the emergency room.

By the time I get clean sheets on the bed, Mama's asleep in her recliner. She looks so peaceful I don't want to wake her, so I climb into her bed and lie there watching her for signs.

Is her breathing too shallow? I ease to her chair and lean close so I can see the movement of her chest. Jefferson whines and I reach down to pat him. "It's okay, boy," I whisper.

Is it?

I climb back into bed and shut my eyes, then instantly pop them open because I've heard a new sound. Is that a gurgle in Mama's chest? Dr. Holman said we could expect more emergencies. Is this one? Creeping in the semidarkness, I stub my toe on her floor lamp, then bite my tongue to keep from saying a word and waking her.

She has twisted in her sleep and tangled the lap robe around her ankles. Rather than risk disturbing her by untangling it, I grab a blanket off the bed so she won't get a chill from the air conditioner. It settles over her, but I still stand by her chair with my toes curled into the rug and my anxious feelings pressing between my shoulders.

Mama opens her eyes. "Maggie, what are you doing here? Is it morning? Is it time for breakfast?"

Oh lord, oh lord…

I tell her what happened and she says, "I forgot, that's all." Her hair is matted and her blue eyes are glassy and I don't know what to do.

"Help me into bed, and then go back to sleep, Maggie."

"I'll stay here, Mama. In this chair."

"I don't want you in here. You snore."

After I've settled her back in bed, I lie between my own cool sheets with my eyes wide open and my mind filled with a dozen possibilities: *I'm wrong, the doctor's right, Mama's feisty act has fooled us all, she's really leaving us, leaving me...and oh, lord, selfish me, does this setback mean I won't have to sit at Jean's dining-room table with Stanley cutting his roast beef into exact little cubes, and Charlie kicking off his shoes and running his sock feet up my leg?*

There's a fine line between being cooperative and gracious and being a doormat. Lately I've been flinging myself on the floor and posting signs saying Step On Me. I'm fixing to change that. First thing in the morning, I'm calling Jean to cancel the party. Mama's certainly not up to it...and neither am I.

Mama beat me to it. She called Jean at the crack of dawn to spin her own version of the night's events and to threaten a hunger strike if the dinner party was canceled.

The only bright spot in this scenario is that I don't have to drive Jean to the grocery store and pick out

Stanley's roast. Aunt Mary Quana is arriving late this afternoon and she'll be Jean's transportation while she's here.

Aunt Mary Quana is a watered-down, primped-up version of Mama. Sitting on Jean's sofa in a pink feathered straw hat and black patent-leather pumps, a matching purse on her lap and her ankles crossed the way she was taught ladies do, she's bound and determined to mind my business or burst her girdle trying.

"Victoria tells me Stanley is coming to dinner, and I can't tell you how much that pleases me. Why, if I had another chance with my Larry I'd be so happy I'd turn cartwheels and shoot poots at the moon."

Well…I didn't say she wasn't sassy.

"I divorced him, Aunt Mary Quana. I don't want him back."

"Neglect your rose petals and your bloom fades quickly," she says.

Good grief. Aunt Mary Quana, too? I have to show them I don't need any help with my neglected "rose petals." If I wanted a man, I could get one all by myself. Couldn't I?

Mentally I go through the list of men I know, men I can call and invite to the dinner party, men who will wear white shirts and pressed jeans and the clean, fresh-air aroma of Irish Spring soap. All I can come up with is Newton Cramer. A kind, harmless old gentleman who would bring yellow-centered daisies and kiss my hand—which leaves out my more interesting body parts.

A new idea presents itself, one too crazy to contemplate, too wild and unexpected.

And perfect. *Maybe*.

Before I can change my mind, I say, "I have to go home to check my phone messages. To see if my editor has called." Mama and Jean exchange looks that say, *Why doesn't she use her cell phone or Jean's phone?* "And I have a few letters I need to type. Business." I grab my purse and fish out my keys. "I'll be back after a while."

Driving back to Mama's in the early dusk, I turn on the radio hoping for a fortifying talk with Rainman, but all I get is a whiskey-voiced DJ who welcomes me to an afternoon of Mississippi blues, starting with "Stop Arguing Over Me" by Eddie Cusic. Some people don't know that Eddie laid his guitar down for twenty-five years while he worked in a rock quarry to support his family, and then picked it up again when he retired and continued making music as if he'd never stopped.

I know because of Stanley. During the lonely married years when he preferred the company of golfing buddies to the company of his wife, and I preferred anything to the judgmental presence of my husband, I spent my dancing-loving-laughing energies on reading stacks of magazines and books on everything that interested me. And blues topped the list.

In a last-ditch effort at togetherness, I even planned a weekend in Cleveland at the Delta Blues Festival, but Stanley killed that idea because he said the Mississippi Delta had mosquitoes as big as Thanksgiving turkeys and heat that would make him break out in hives under the waistband of his Fruit of the Looms.

Parked in the deep shade of Mama's magnolia tree, fishing around in my purse for his business card, I send a prayer winging toward the silver goddess moon that Rainman answers…and that he's not allergic to heat.

Of any kind.

I dial and when he answers, I'm embarrassed and tongue-tied and three seconds away from hanging up the phone.

"Hello…is anybody there?"

No, nobody I want to say, because Mama taught me it's bad manners to hang up without saying anything. But then I remember that I *am* there, and that I'm Somebody and I'm fighting very hard to stay that way.

"This is Maggie…Maggie Dufrane."

"The writer with the great smile."

He makes it easy to invite him to dinner, easy to be happy when he says yes.

Afterward I pull down the rearview mirror so I can confirm or deny my *great smile*. It's there, and it's kind of nice. I tilt the mirror lower for a better view. Actually, it's great. It really is.

I would never have known that about myself if I had hung up. The call becomes my three seconds to grace, and I roll down my window and look at the moon, smiling and smiling.

Eventually I'll go back to Jean's because we're having a pajama party at her house in honor of Aunt Mary Quana. This is a tradition among the women in our family. A girls' night in. Pajamas and popcorn and pink foam hair curlers (Aunt Mary Quana). Cards and Kahlúa and conversation that ranges from the Republicans (Mama) to Geritol and Viagra (both of them.)

But first I get Jefferson out of his kennel and then go inside to think up a letter to type because I said I would. He prances around the house, sniffing to make sure I'm safe, and then plops beside my feet as I turn on my computer.

I pick up my small stack of mail that now comes to Mama's box and spread it across the dining-room table—a flyer from Home Depot advertising a close-out sale on roses, an application from Citibank for a Diamond Preferred charge card and a bill for $13.98 from McRae's for the pink lipstick Jean charged last month because she'd left her card in her other purse.

This is a depressing display. This is the kind of mail that says I'm vanishing bit by bit, a woman no longer qualified for electric bills, car payments, invitations for two—Mr. and Mrs.—and exorbitant credit-card charges that say this woman decided to go on a spree so she flew to New York, stayed at the Algonquin, splurged on tickets to Broadway shows and took off her shoes at the Metropolitan Museum of Art because it's better to view Picasso's *Les Demoiselles d'Avignon* barefoot.

I open a clean document and type:

Dear Sir:
Congratulations on your beautiful advertising flier. The roses looked so enticing I could hardly resist racing to Home Depot and buying six. Alas, I don't have time for gardening—even if I had one—because I'm always in my car.
Sincerely yours,
Maggie Dufrane

I press Save and try to lean back in Mama's straight-backed dining-room chair, but all I can manage is a neck-crimping slump. Maybe I'll mail the letter. After all, everybody needs affirmation. Even Home Depot.

After I put Jefferson in his kennel, I drive back to Jean's. She and Mama are already in pajamas, and Aunt Mary Quana's in a nightgown that reads Keep America Beautiful, Put a Sack Over Your Head. It's pink, an exact match to her fuzzy house shoes, her fingernail polish and the foam-rubber rollers in her hair.

"It's about time you got here," Mama says. "We can't play Rook without you."

Aunt Mary Quana grabs the cards and starts shuffling, but Mama snatches them out of her hand. "I'm dealing, Mary Quana. You always cheat."

"How do you know?"

"Because I taught you."

I wish I could wrap pink tissue paper around this moment and put it in a box on my closet shelf. It would be the kind of box that could transport you through time and space, a miraculous box you could climb into and fly backward to the beauty of a sister with tears of laughter streaming down her face, an aunt who would drive her car to China if somebody could figure a way to put a bridge across the ocean, and a mama with devilment in her eyes and age spots on her hands.

* * *

I wait until Jean and I are alone before I tell her about Rainman. We're sitting in the middle of her cherry four-poster bed, listening to the twin freight-train snores of Mama and Aunt Mary Quana. It's one in the morning, a good time for sisters to share secrets and confess crimes.

Jean narrows her lips at the news of her extra dinner guest, an expression she learned from Mama. Finally she says, "Maggie, is he a good man?"

"So far, so good."

"I just want you to have the same things I do—a home, security and a wonderful man to love."

"It's way too early for that. Besides, I know only one wonderful man, and you've already got him."

"Lucky me. Look, Maggie, I didn't mean to goad you about your neglected sex drive. I'm sorry."

"It's okay. I plan to make you pay for it." I wallop her with the feather pillow and she grabs hers to fight back. We're children again, full of giggles and spontaneity and the absolute certainty that the world will never break our hearts.

But it does.

"Jean, Maggie," Mama calls.

My sister and I leap off the bed and collide in the narrow hallway trying to answer her late-night alarm.

Mama's doubled over on the side of the bed with her head on her knees. We race across the room and flank her, bookends of sympathy and fear. Between groans, Mama finally requests Pepto-Bismol. We press for doctors and the emergency room, but she's adamant that it's nothing but indigestion.

"You might as well hush about the hospital. I'm not fixing to upset Mary Quana," Mama says.

While Jean and I rummage through her medicine cabinet, we agree that judging by the decibel level coming from Aunt Mary Quana's room, it would take a level-four hurricane to disturb her.

CHAPTER 10

Venus is putting on a show tonight, folks. All you young lovers should make some time to sit under the stars, and if you've been with each other a while, and already do a lot of porch sitting, well, hold hands while you're at it.
—*Rainman*

Mama and I are headed to Jean's for the dinner party. A gathering that will probably turn out to resemble something staged by the Three Stooges. Jean so nervous she's fixed every casserole known to man. Aunt Mary Quana wearing feathers and high expectations. Stanley basking in the company of my family. Charlie casting baleful glances toward Rainman. And Mama, fortified on stubbornness and Pepto-Bismol, running the show.

I picture the way Rainman will see me tonight—a middle-aged woman in a hopeful pink blouse and black slacks because no woman past a certain age and in a certain weight category would dare put anything except black or navy on her hips. A woman with flying-every-which-way Orphan Annie hair that refuses to be tamed and lipstick that doesn't match, trying too hard to strike the right balance between intelligence and wittiness.

A woman trying too hard. Period.

I wish I were in Mama's dream red convertible. I would be on the way to someplace grand wearing pink chiffon and discreet pearls. I'd glide through the ballroom striking awe and admiration into the heart of every person there. Whispers would follow me as I waltzed onto the dance floor, *Who is she?*

"Maggie...you passed Jean's driveway."

Who I am is a woman losing her mind and her nerve at the same time. Lord, why didn't I merely endure an evening with Stanley and Charlie and leave Rainman at the radio station?

"What were you thinking?" Mama adds.

"I was thinking that we should have canceled this dinner party two days ago when you got so sick at Jean's house. You're not up to this, and neither am I."

I'm sleep-deprived, harried and worried. Darkness is a signal for every organ in Mama's body to rise up in protest. Each night brings a new pain, a new problem, a new way to test my ingenuity at home remedies. I'm so exhausted from nighttime nursing duties that when I sit down to write, I fall asleep with my head on the unopened computer.

"Flitter, speak for yourself. And perk up. I don't want to eat Jean's roast beef across from a sourpuss."

"Then you'd better put Charlie on your side of the table."

"Be nice to him. One evening in his company is not going to kill you."

"That which doesn't kill me makes me stronger."

"Quit quoting. I can't stand it when you do that. Especially when I don't know who said it."

"Camus first, I think, and then that guy who wrote *Steel Magnolias*. I can't remember his name."

"If I'd wanted to have dinner with an encyclopedia, I'd have brought one…. Wait. Slow down. You can turn around in Laura Kate's driveway."

If it were left up to me, I'd keep on going. From years of being the only driver in this family, I know these back roads as well as I know the café-au-lait-colored birthmark on my left knee. I could drive clear to Florida, never taking a major highway. Mama and I would lie on the beaches of Pensacola Bay and let the sun burn away every sick and fearful thing until nothing was left except clean, pure space.

When we pull up in Jean's driveway, Mama says, "Smile, Charlie's here."

In a way, this is a good thing because now, when Rainman comes, I won't give the appearance of a woman alone and looking, one of those female predators you can spot the minute you enter a crowded room, the one laughing too loudly, and staying too long. And I hope I remember to call Rainman by his real name. What if I spill gravy on my blouse or get lettuce caught between my teeth? What if I say the same silly things to him in person that I've said for the last three months when he was nothing more than a voice on the radio?

I fade into my family and wait. This is easy to do: wherever Mama is, she's the center of the show. And Aunt Mary Quana runs a close second. While Jean keeps Horton and Hattie and Laura Kate talking, they surround Stanley, and I can tell by the supercilious grin on his face that he thinks they've rolled out the welcome mat especially for him. He seems to have forgotten that Mama and Aunt Mary Quana pour on the charm for everybody, even people they don't like. It's their generation's Southern way. Win them over with honey and wait for your chance to cut out their hearts.

Mama sees me and nods toward Charlie standing in the corner tugging at his ugly brown tie. If I didn't know why she was doing this, I'd be mad at her. Instead, my heart is filled with gratitude and a wavery sort of courage because I know that whatever happens to me, Mama's still there trying to make things better. She's too smart not to know how her own body is betraying her, and she probably views this as a last chance to help.

Mama can't stand to see her daughters lack for anything, and that includes a husband. In my case, she's seeing a once-secure, once-successful daughter reduced to living with her mother.

Charlie finally works up his courage and joins me. "Maggie, how are you?"

"Fine." I give him the standard reply Southern women give when they don't want to talk to you. A polite go away. Charlie doesn't take the hint, so I say, "Thank you for coming to Aunt Mary Quana's welcome party. I know you'll want to spend lots of time with her."

"I came for *you*, Maggie. Let's go out on the patio where we can talk."

The reason I don't simply tell him no is that I'm not good at public refusals. I'm too soft, too aware of other people's viewpoints, too anxious about hurting feelings. There are words for people like me, none of them nice—pushover, wishy-washy, doormat.

Suddenly the doorbell rings and I am saved.

"Excuse me, please," I tell Charlie. "That will be my guest. My *special* guest."

Sometimes, when you least expect it, there's grace. And he's standing on Jean's front stoop wearing a white shirt, sleeves rolled, and the soap-fresh scent of Irish Spring. I don't know why I find that combination so appealing. Certainly Stanley never rolled his sleeves, even in the days when he was my hero. Plus, he's a Dial soap man and always follows that with too much after-shave, a strong scent that walks into the room before he does.

Rainman reaches for my hand. "Hello again, Maggie."

Suddenly I'm aware of every bit of fluff on my hips. I'm going to sue Hershey's. If it weren't for five extra chocolate pounds, I'd feel charming and self-confident and skinny. Well, maybe ten, but I'm not admitting an ounce more.

Or maybe I'll thank them because men like Rainman who can walk into a room and fit right into a crazy family like mine have no business in my life. I don't need the distraction, I'm too busy trying to steer my derailed train.

Steer is putting it mildly. I can't even find the track. Jean marches by with a steaming platter of cornbread. "Joe, you sit here between Mama and Aunt Mary Quana, and Maggie you sit over there by your husband."

"Ex," I say, and Rainman takes notice. I can tell by the way his mouth curves. Not quite a smile, certainly not a grin, just a pleasant expression that would be easy to live with. Too easy.

While Stanley drones on about the number of tax returns he prepared this season, and Charlie readjusts his tie over his Adam's apple and tries to catch my eye, Rainman is telling Mama about carving Victorian roses on a cherrywood chair.

"Furniture-making is my hobby," he says.

His hands are smooth and olive-skinned with wonderfully curved thumbs, and I picture them running down the length of a cherry leg, smoothing and polishing. His are the kind of hands that can create a finely turned piece of furniture or slice roast beef with careless ease or mend a broken heart.

Not that Stanley broke mine, not entirely, but no matter how much you want a relationship to end, there's a little piece of your heart that says, *Wait, this is familiar, if I leave who will I talk to, who will I build memories with, where will I put my cold feet when I'm searching for a warm spot underneath the covers on a chilly December morning?*

Rainman would make cold feet a moot point because how could any part of you be cold with hands like that all over your body? Hands that can carve a rose?

Hands that belong to somebody with a brain? Lord, now he's talking to Mama about poetry. Elizabeth Barrett Browning. Love poems.

Who will I love? That's what the split-apart heart wants to know, and here sits a man who speaks of love at the dinner table.

Charlie makes a beeline for me after dinner, but Rainman smoothly cuts him off. Taking my arm, he says, "Maggie, will you show me your sister's place? I haven't seen a lake like that since I left Chicago."

I could kiss his feet. Instead I settle for enjoying the delicious tingle in my arm where his hand touches. We slip through the French doors and into the moonlight.

"Thank you." I step apart, expecting him to let go, but, oh, he doesn't, and I feel attractive and desirable and giddy all at the same time.

"No problem." I like it that he doesn't make a negative comment about Charlie. This shows character, an old-fashioned virtue, hard to find.

The lake in the moonlight is one of the most romantic places on the farm. Did Rainman pick it deliberately?

"When I was sixteen I wrote a poem about a lake," he says. "Lake Michigan." *Yes, yes.*

"This one doesn't compare."

"But it does. It's not the size but the feelings. There's something about a lake in moonlight that makes you think you can have everything you want, whether it's a different life or just a lazy evening fishing."

He slides his hand down my arm, twines his fingers through mine. "What do you want, Maggie?"

This list is short and mundane, but I don't say, a contract, a mortgage and a dog of my own because he hasn't asked that kind of question. What I say is, "Magic."

He kisses my hand, just that, but it feels like more, and we stand at the lakeside with the moment pulsing between us while we watch the venturing moon leave silver tracks across the water.

Finally this word-struck man with the talented hands says he has to go, and I escort him to his car. "Thank you for inviting me, Maggie. I don't often get to be part of a family gathering."

Why? I wonder, but I don't ask. I don't want him to think I'm interested. Well…I *am*, but not in a personal sort of way that would lead to dinner for two and music in the moonlight and crisp white shirts on the floor.

Currently I'm a ship with a hole in its hull, not the kind you'd want to climb aboard and set sail with.

"I'm glad you could come," I say.

"I'd like to see you again. Friday night? Dinner…for two this time."

Does he read minds? I hope not. In spite of my wrecked-ship condition, mine is tangled on the floor with his white shirt and his briefs. Skimpy ones. Black. I know because no man with long, muscular legs like his would be caught dead in boxers.

I would wear something soft and feminine, a crinkled silk broomstick skirt, rose-colored like the carvings on his furniture, and I'd go bare-legged, toenails painted shiny vermillion. Maybe I'd put glitter polish on top so it would look like I'm walking among stars.

Yes is what I'm thinking, but I say, "Mama's health is not good, and I'm taking care of her right now." Does he think I'm making excuses, that he's not my type? It's been so long I don't even know if I have a type.

Neither of us moves. Do I shake his hand? Turn and go into the house? What? I feel old and out of practice, an Edsel that got scrapped because it was a market dud, a bad idea, a terrible design.

Suddenly I feel Rainman's hand in my hair, and he's

twining one untamed curl around his finger. "Some other time," he replies, and then he's gone.

Oh… I never even told him that sometimes he's the only person I can talk to.

"Maggie, are you still out there?" Jean is calling to me from inside her house, and when she steps onto the porch with me, the moonlight makes her hair look like fairy dust. "What are you doing?"

"I don't know," I say. "Just breathing."

"It feels good, doesn't it?"

Jean kicks off her shoes, and we stand side by side looking up at the stars. Without the competition of city lights, they're so brilliant they seem to burn in the night sky. A huge advantage of country living.

Another is the night sounds. Instead of the hum and drone of traffic outside my apartment window, I hear the summer song of cicadas, the violin chirp of crickets and the deep bass note of a big bullfrog in the pond south of Jean's house.

"The guests have all gone," Jean says.

"I know. I can't go back in just yet. I need some time to think."

"About Joe? He seems like a nice guy."

"I don't have time for men. I've got to do a writer's

workshop. Earn a little money. I can't continue living on Mama's charity."

"It's not charity. We're family. And you'd better not let Mama hear you say that. She'd kill you."

"She probably will anyhow. We'd better get back in there."

Mama and Aunt Mary Quana are having a big argument—they call it a discussion—about whether Mama ought to go to Atlanta and live with her sister in the Golden Age Retirement Home.

"I've got my own house, Mary Quana, and I'm not fixing to give it up to live with a bunch of old farts who eat prunes for breakfast."

"You'd better be careful who you call names, Victoria. For your information, I'm the only one of us driving."

"I've got Maggie…and Walter, when he's here."

Instead of getting into the middle of this fray, I excuse myself, go into the kitchen and start pouring coffee. Decaf because I don't want insomnia.

By the time I get back to the den with coffee, Jean's sitting in Walter's recliner biting her fingernails and Mama and Aunt Mary Quana are sitting on opposite sides of the room not speaking.

"Let's all drink and make up," I say.

"Nothing wrong with me," Mama argues. "It's Mary Quana who's got her nose out of joint."

"Well, all right," Aunt Mary Quana says. "Put a little Jack Daniel's in there, and I'll drink to that."

Jean fetches the bottle and, while Aunt Mary Quana is getting tipsy and Mama's falling asleep in her chair, we slip into the kitchen to do dishes.

"Maggie, will you be all right with Mama and Aunt Mary Quana for a few days? Walter's flying into San Francisco, and wants me to join him."

Her face is flushed and her skin shines as if it has been polished with Ajax. Desire winds around the kitchen like a strangler fig, and I have a hard time keeping my mind off a pair of fine olive-skinned hands on a clean white shirt, popping buttons and ripping aside restraints.

"Go ahead, Jean. Have a big time. We'll be fine."

Aunt Mary Quana goes home with us, following my Jeep in her outrageous Caddy, and it's midnight before I get them settled into bed.

At two o'clock, I startle awake with a unicorn dancing through my head. Dream? Prophecy? Past-life memory? He's so real, so splendid and still so vivid that I know he's important.

I snap on the light, and by the time I've found my

bedside notepad, I already know what he is—the beginning of an idea, a magnificent science-fiction/fantasy that's nothing like my cozy cat mysteries.

With everything blocked out except the words that tumble forth so fast my hand can barely keep up, I scribble until the first pink fingers of dawn touch my windowsill.

CHAPTER 11

July is coming in with a bang, folks. As my grand-
daddy used to say, it's raining cats and dogs out
there. Man, what a storm. Don't drive in it unless you have to.

—*Rainman*

Jean has been in San Francisco only four days, and
here I am on a midnight run to the emergency room.
Mama's in the back seat in a nest of blankets and pillows and Aunt Mary Quana's perched on the edge of
the passenger seat like a small yellow bird fixing to take
flight. Her yellow terry bathrobe is unbelted, yellow
fuzzy-duck slippers beating a tattoo on the floorboard
and yellow nightshirt declaring Who Made You
Queen? I Didn't Resign.

"Go a little faster, Maggie," she says. "Lord, we're
never going to make it at this speed."

Mama raises herself from the pile of pillows on the back seat and says, "Mary Quana, will you shut up? I'm the one dying here, not you."

Fifteen minutes ago, when I found Mama heaving on the side of the bed, she asked for the doctor instead of Pepto-Bismol.

I called Dr. Holman, and he's waiting for us at the hospital.

"Gallstones," he finally tells us.

"Cut me open and take them out," Mama says.

"Let's get you in a room tonight and get you comfortable."

"I'm sick and tired of putting up with these old things. Lately I've been sick as a dog. Go ahead and get them out."

"We'll discuss options tomorrow," he says, and for once, Mama doesn't talk back. But only because the pain medication has taken effect and she's falling asleep.

While the staff settles Mama into a room and Aunt Mary Quana's occupied with a cup of coffee, I have a private talk with Dr. Holman.

"This is serious, Maggie. The gallstones could go into her bile duct and cause pancreatitis, which could be fatal. But with her weakened heart, the surgery might also kill her."

I feel as if I'm climbing a mountain with no end in sight.

"She's strong-willed and determined," I tell him. "Doesn't that count for something?"

"It does. Still, the risks of surgery are monumental." He pats my hand. "You look tired, Maggie. Sleep on it."

"I will."

But first I have to climb another little hill—call Jean, which I dread. Problems have a way of getting inside her and eating her alive. To thrive, she requires "normal."

I don't even know what that is anymore.

I dial her cell phone, and when she answers, sounding perky and rested, I almost say, *I was planning to do a workshop two weeks from Tuesday, and I just wanted to confirm that you'll be home to take care of Mama.*

But then, what if they do surgery and Mama dies? Jean would never forgive me.

I tell her about the seriousness of Mama's current situation, leaving out the part that she might not survive. I won't let myself think about that.

"Walter and I will get the next flight out…." Jean's crying. I can tell. "Maggie…did you hear me? I'm coming home."

My sister's words let me slump against the wall,

drained. How do you accept a situation that is intolerable? How do you keep on putting one foot in front of the other when the only person who knows the road is drifting slowly away and might not come back?

"Maggie." Aunt Mary Quana is standing in the doorway of Mama's room. "Are you coming in?"

"Just a minute," I say, and it's only after she goes back inside that I realize I'm crying, too.

I wipe my face, take a deep breath and tell myself, *Buck up, Mama's in there fighting and so should you.* Then I push open the heavy door and walk through.

There's a word for what I'm doing. It's called faith. And sometimes it's the only thing that lets you go on.

At 5:00 a.m. I leave Aunt Mary Quana snoring in the lounge chair beside Mama's bed and drive home to take care of Jefferson. The radio dial is still set to WTUP. When I hear Rainman saying, "It's going to be a nice day today, folks. Plenty of sunshine after the big storm last night. Don't forget the big Fourth of July celebration at Ballard Park. WTUP will be there all day, broadcasting."

I could use a celebration—brass bands and marching music, red-white-and-blue cabanas and Rainman smelling of Irish Spring soap, charming the crowd—and me—with his patter.

There's a wistfulness in this kind of thinking, a sadness that feels as if I'm in mourning. And maybe I am. My coming-alive feelings are withering from neglect.

Rainman plays something jumpy and nerve-wracking that jerks me out of the doldrums, hip-hop stuff by a recording artist who probably has a name like Ham and Jam or Big Bad Mama.

My own mama looked so pale and small lying under the white hospital sheets. Faded. Like a photograph that's been left in the sun, the picture slowly bleaching until all that's left is an outline, a faint shadow of the vibrant person who once occupied the frame.

I switch the radio off because even if Rainman had called, I'd have said no. It's lovely having him as a disembodied voice, somebody who listens to my problems and never judges, never overreacts no matter what I say. He's like a pen pal in Switzerland or New Zealand, somebody I've been corresponding with for years, a distant friend who understands. Always.

Well… It's a darned good thing I turned his dinner invitation down because he'd have a hard time living up to that fantasy.

I park the Jeep under Mama's magnolia tree and go to the kennel to tell Jefferson about Mama. Not that he doesn't already know. Dogs have a sixth sense about these things.

His ears are flattened and his mouth is drooping in mournful lines. I lean down, wrap my arms around him and press my face into his fur. He smells like kennel dust and summer sunshine and loyalty. He smells like home.

I want to take him into Mama's house and lie down beside him on the rug, put my head on his chest and fall asleep with the sound of his big, solid heartbeat in my ear. I want to forget about hospitals and emergency rooms and surgeries that can destroy battered, worn-out hearts.

I need a break. I don't want to think about tanked careers and shrinking bank accounts and failed relationships and workshops that might net enough to plug a small hole in the dam but will do nothing to shore up the walls and stop the plummeting flood of finances.

Inside, I check my e-mails and run my fingers across the items on my day planner: call editor, assemble workshop notes, check want ads for temp job, create unicorn file. The last notation is my shorthand way of launching a novel that burst into flame the night Rainman came to Jean's dinner party. I'm raring to write, itching to tap into that beautiful flow, but, oh, I can barely keep my eyes open.

I lie on Mama's sofa and close my eyes, just for a moment, while Jefferson stretches on the rug beside me. When he jars me awake with feet-flailing, mock-bark dreams of chasing rabbits, I slump with my head in my hands, groggy and guilty. Good daughters don't sleep while sickness stalks their mothers.

I ease up so I won't wake him, then go into Mama's room to pack her good nightgowns, the ones she saves for special occasions. I want to open my mouth and scream until I'm hoarse. Nobody's special occasion should be the hospital.

By four o'clock, Jean and Walter are back from San Francisco, and we all gather in Mama's hospital room to discuss options.

Mama's sitting up, her color partially restored. I don't know whether it's from medication or a reflection of her red gown. Whatever the source, she's revived enough to put an end to our endless agonizing over whether she should risk surgery.

"I'm having it," she says. "It's my body, and I'll do what I want to. You might as well not say another word."

And so we don't.

CHAPTER 12

It's another sunny day in July, and if you didn't catch the Independence Day celebration at Ballard Park, you missed a treat.

—*Rainman*

"**We** didn't catch it, Rainman," I tell him, "but we have another reason to celebrate. Mama made it through her surgery…and she's already home."

Jean stops biting her fingernails long enough to reach over and turn off the radio. I expect her to give me a look, or even a lecture, but she merely sits in the passenger side of the Jeep staring out the window.

"Are you depressed because Walter's gone again?" Ireland this time, I think.

"No."

"Well, you're going to have to perk up and tell me where to turn. We're fixing to hit the first red light, and

I need to know where we're going. And it had better not be Eternal Rest Funeral Home. I'm not in the mood to casket hunt."

"Wal-Mart. And that's all I'm saying."

I drive Jean to Wal-Mart all the time while Walter's out of town. Why should picking up toilet paper make her look as if she's just witnessed the massacre of elephants for their ivory tusks?

When she called this morning, I was giving Mama a bath. "Light candles, Maggie," she told me. "Put on a CD. I want to celebrate coming home again."

Although she was not in the tub, merely sitting on a bath chair while I sponged her, I lit candles all around—rose-scented, pink and rose and ruby-red candles that cast both of us in flattering light while Eric Clapton crooned "Wonderful Tonight." When he came to the line about brushing your long blond hair, Mama said, "I might get a wig."

"You've got plenty of hair and it's not even gray." This is her Cherokee heritage, this thick black hair that's barely sprinkled with silver.

"Yes, but it's not blond."

"Why on earth would you want to go blond?"

"Maybe I'm fixing to kick up my heels and have an affair."

That's when Jean called, and it's a good thing, because Mama was acting so serious I believed her.

"Aren't you going to answer the phone?" she asked.

"I don't know whether to leave you or not. There's no telling what you'll do next."

"Go on, Maggie. Get the phone. It might be somebody important."

"Your mystery man?"

"I was just kidding. Since your daddy died there hasn't been a man who could hold a candle to him."

Now Mama's sitting in her recliner playing a game of gin rummy with Aunt Mary Quana—cheating, no doubt—while I park the Jeep and follow Jean into Wal-Mart.

When I told Mama this is where I'd be going, she said, "You might as well get some handicapped rails for the bathtub." Then she picked up her crossword puzzle book and started filling in blanks as if she'd suggested I pick up something insignificant, such as potato chips.

If I think about what Mama's latest request means, I'll start crying. I can't even bear to talk about it with Jean. Instead I say, "I'll meet you up front. In…say, half an hour?"

"No. I want you with me." She heads toward the

pharmacy, and I have to trot to keep up. "I can't do this without you."

"Do what?" I ask, and she reaches to the shelf and grabs an early-pregnancy test kit.

"Good grief."

"It's probably nothing. Stress. It's not unusual to miss a couple of periods at my age."

Ten minutes later we're huddled in the disabled bathroom stall at Wal-Mart's, watching the little stick Jean peed on to see what color it turns.

Blue. She throws it into the air and goes into hysterics.

"Maggie, what are we going to do?"

We? I'm not the one pregnant here. I haven't even been exposed, if she'll care to remember. Not that I want to be. A busy woman like me. Running the Lucas show.

Still, desire has a way of sneaking up on you. For instance, when you're in the kitchen at midnight, raiding the pantry for peanut butter and crackers because you can't sleep and there's nobody in bed to help you. Or you're standing in the moonlight, inhaling the clean, soap-scrubbed scent of a broad-shouldered man wearing Irish Spring.

Jean's histrionics send passion scuttling.

I reach in my purse and hand her a tissue. "We'll

have an ob-gyn check this out. What we're not going to do is stand in a public-bathroom stall screaming and crying."

"Was I?"

"Yes. Stop it," I say, and she does.

On the way to the car, I notice children everywhere—sitting in strollers with drool on their chins, climbing their mothers' legs with chocolate-smeared hands, poking holes in a bag of flour and dancing in the powdery white trail while their mothers wheel the grocery cart across the parking lot, unaware.

Jean and I both wanted children. She was going to have four—two boys and two girls—and I was going to have three—sex unimportant. We sat up nearly all night on the eve of her wedding discussing what our children would look like and what we'd name them. "Victoria, for my first girl," she said, and I told her that if Stanley ever got up the nerve to propose and I got pregnant first, I was going to use that name. I pictured a little girl with my big hair and Mama's big attitude.

But Baby Victoria remained a dream. Neither of us got pregnant. After six years, Stanley and I quit trying, partially because we got so busy we didn't see how children would fit into our lifestyle, but mostly because we lost interest in the baby-making process.

Jean quit trying seven years ago. "It's self-centered

of us to go on this way when there are so many children out there needing good homes," is what she told me. And then a few months later she said they'd decided not to adopt because of Walter's travel.

Obviously, though, she and Walter never lost interest in *the process*.

No wonder they call envy the green-eyed monster. Here I am driving my car while it's clawing away at my insides. Or maybe that's fear. *Lord, lord...* Jean's past the normal child-bearing age. What if her eggs are not up to snuff?

And Walter's forty-six. Good grief...I hate to think of the tired condition of his Y chromosomes.

"We won't tell Walter and Mama until I know for sure," Jean says.

"Certainly not."

No use in everybody worrying. Or celebrating. Or falling apart.

Jean turns her face to the window and cries without sound. I don't offer a tissue because something in the set of her shoulders tells me that this time she wants to be inside herself, alone.

After I take her home, I turn the Jeep around and head back into town. And then I stand in front of the display of disabled rails, crying.

"Is anything wrong, ma'am?"

The clerk is wearing a name tag that reads Tewanda Hardy. She looks so sweet-faced and sincere that I want to take her to lunch and pour out my story just so she can reach across the table and pat my hand.

Instead I say, "There's a bug in my eye."

She reaches into her pocket and hands me a travel pack of tissue and, after I thank her, I ask if the rails come with their own screws and installing instructions.

"It has everything you need," she tells me. "You can do it."

And I say, "Yes," because I know I can. I *must*.

When I leave the hubbub of the store, I hear my cell phone beep. It's probably another frantic message from Jean or Mama. I don't want to listen to it until I'm in the car sitting down. I'm all out of problem-solving gas.

"Maggie, this is Joe," my voice mail says, and suddenly my tank is full. "I thought you might need a little break. If so, join me at the Malco at four for *Monster-in-Law*.

I sit in the car and argue with myself: You need to put up disabled rails. Yes, but everybody needs a break, and you can put up rails tonight... *Look, Rainman could be a serious distraction and you don't have time to be sidetracked and sizzled. But this is not a real date, just two hours at a comedy, and doesn't everybody need to laugh?*

Before I can change my mind, I call Aunt Mary Quana to say that I have a few errands to do for my-self and won't be home till six-thirty. Well…this is only a small white lie, but it's justified because I *do* need to do this one small thing for myself, and I want my stolen afternoon to be just for me, not a shared event that everybody in the family will discuss.

I glance in my rearview mirror, apply fresh lipstick, decide my hair is hopeless and then head northwest to-ward the mall. There's a vacant spot by Joe's car, and the Rainman himself is standing under the marquee watching for me.

When was the last time somebody made me impor-tant enough to wait for, to stand in the blistering July heat and hope that I might get his message and join him?

"There you are." Pleasure and promise are tangled in his greeting, and I walk into the theater with the confident swing of a woman with revved-up hormones and Somebody Special who appreciates them.

"Popcorn?" he asks, and when I nod, we both say, "With lots of butter," and then look at each other as if we've discovered the moon.

"I enjoy movies," Joe says when we settle into mid-theater seats.

"So do I. This is one of my favorite pastimes."

For me, books and movies are inextricably linked. I'm not merely sitting in the dark waiting to be entertained: I've entered a magical world and am waiting to be transported.

And I am, *I am*. Not only by what I'm seeing on the screen but by accidental touching of buttery fingers inside a popcorn box, by strong, jean-clad legs stretched out beside mine. There's a lovely level of comfort between us, and yet awareness, too—not the stuff of fairy tales but a strong sense of *yes, this is right*.

When the monster-in-law finally gets her comeuppance, we roar with laughter, and then smile at each other, a bit self-conscious, a whole lot intrigued.

I'm sorry to see the lights come up. "Thanks, Joe. I needed that break."

"I thought you might. Call me when you need another one."

Then he kisses my palm and folds my fingers over, and I feel like crying, crying for what I'm missing, crying for what I want, crying for the simple beauty of that one small gesture.

Jean and I become sisters with secrets. Three days after the future Baby Lucas flew the blue warning flag in Wal-Mart's toilet and I escaped to the simplicity of shared popcorn and laughter, we're standing in Mama's kitchen tearing spinach for salads and making furtive plans.

"Do you think Aunt Mary Quana will still be here to stay with Mama for my doctor's appointment?" Jean says.

"I'll call Hattie Grimes to come over, just in case." I select rich red radishes for my salad, but leave it out of the rest because I'm the only family member who will eat them. "When's Walter coming home?"

"Not for another two weeks. Lord, what if I'm really pregnant? He's never home. You and Mama will have to move in with me."

My future unfolds, a series of appointments with every major doctor's group in town—surgeons, heart specialists, gynecologists and pediatricians. And in between trips, I'm caretaker, nanny and resident shoulder-to-cry-on. The indispensable woman. Loved, respected, needed and desired. But certainly not by Somebody Wonderful in fly-front jeans.

How would I ever fit him in? Pun absolutely intended.

I could be overwhelmed if I weren't so busy chopping cucumbers and green onions.

"I think I'll just cancel my writers' workshop."

"You will not. You need the income, Maggie. And besides, you need to get away."

Yes. To a nice beach house in Tahiti where I'll spend my days wading in the surf, collecting seashells, napping in a tree-swung hammock and drinking from a coconut shell filled with cool beverages, preferably alcoholic.

What Jean doesn't understand—or anybody else not in this business, for that matter—is that teaching a workshop is not "getting away." It's what the name implies. *Work*.

And yet it is energizing and satisfying in its own way. Talking about something I love. Imparting ten years of accumulated expertise. Interacting with artistic types.

I don't explain any of that to Jean, though. She has enough to worry about. What I say is "Okay, I won't cancel." What I do is keep slicing fresh vegetables. Life goes on, one cucumber at a time.

"Maggie, come quick." Aunt Mary Quana's in the doorway with one shoe on and one shoe off. "Victoria's having a heart attack."

Jean and I bolt, almost knocking Aunt Mary Quana off her black-patent pump. Mama's bent over in a blue velvet wing chair, coughing.

Jean grabs the phone while I put my arms around Mama's shoulders.

"Are you all right?" I say, and Mama bolts upright.

"What on earth are you doing?"

"Calling 911," Jean says. "Aunt Mary Quana said you're dying."

"Put that phone down. I've just got a frog in my throat, that's all." Mama clears her throat, glaring at her sister. "Mary Quana, what are you trying to do? Scare everybody half to death?"

"Well, I guess I know when I've worn out my welcome. I'll be leaving tomorrow."

"Flitter, you were leaving tomorrow anyway. Wild horses couldn't keep you away from the birthday bash that retirement home's throwing for you."

After Mama and Aunt Mary Quana go to bed, I hole up in my bedroom and start capturing my unicorn in a new file while he's still fresh. Words pour through my fingertips, and when the flow finally stops, I go to stand beside the window. The moon is full, and bright patches of light are caught in the tops of trees. In a scene this peaceful, there's no room for a cough that signals a failing heart, no room for a joking, ranting voice to become a frail, breakable thing.

I press my cheek to the night-cooled windowpane and whisper, "*Please, God.*" That's all. Just two words, spoken with a fervent hope.

"Maggie…" Mama calls, and I run.

She's standing beside her bed, hanging on to the bedpost. "Can you help me get to the bathroom?"

This is new, this weakness that won't let her take care of her own nighttime needs.

"Don't tell Jean," she says. "She worries."

Proud. Fierce. That's what I'm thinking as I hold her upright on the toilet.

"I won't, Mama. I promise."

On Tuesday, after Aunt Mary Quana leaves, Jean and I are sitting side by side on a red Chinese-print sofa waiting for Dr. Milton Crawford to come in and tell us the truth about her pregnancy. Jean looks almost nonchalant thumbing through a sleek July edition of *Architectural Digest*. Only a sister could see the tension in her jaw, the way she holds her mouth tight over clenched teeth.

I think about mouths, and how they can tell exactly what a person is feeling. You don't have to say a word, really, just let the shape and contours of your mouth do the talking.

I'm aware of the way my own lips are pressed together, and suddenly it strikes me as sad that news of a brand-new little being coming into this world would cause such turmoil and anxiety. It occurs to me that we make too many judgments, that we label everything in our lives either Good or Bad.

Forget all the reasons why having a baby at the age of forty-three is a bit scary. Forget all the fretting and agonizing and advance planning. Why can't we just let a thing *be?* Why can't we be like Mama?

If she were here, I know what she'd say. "That's the way it is. Make the best of it."

This is a lesson I should apply to my own life. And I will. *I will.* As soon as I get through applying it to Jean's.

Dr. Crawford comes in to deliver the news that my sister's due date is February fifteenth, which sounds about right to me. Jean was cooking up more than hot casseroles that warm May evening when I carried creamed corn to Mama, and Walter carried Jean to bed.

I grab my sister's hand as she walks in numbed silence toward my Jeep. "We'll make the best of it," I tell her, and what I'm thinking is *love*. That's what the best is, and that's all this baby will need. Food and shelter, of course. But most of all love.

When we get in the car, Jean says, "We're not telling till Walter gets back. I want to see his face." And then… "What if I'm so old my milk's gone sour?"

"I don't think age has anything to do with it."

"I don't have a clue about toilet training. You can scar a kid for life with toilet training."

"For Pete's sake, Jean. Let's not borrow trouble."

I'm trying very hard to take my own advice. Janice Whitten hasn't called. (Does she hate my revised proposal? Has she read it? Is it lost?) As soon as I drop off my sister, I'm calling her.

Janice doesn't answer. I leave a message, then take my cell phone into the laundry room and start folding clothes, a pile for Mama, a pile for me. This task requires little brain power and leaves me free to conjure the worst outright rejection and the necessity of finding a job, any old job.

But where? Piggly Wiggly? I can barely operate a handheld can opener, let alone a cash register. The city park? I know CPR and rescue breathing, but I'm a terrible swimmer and I'm downright frightening in a swimsuit.

Buck up, I tell myself, and I do. Because, here's the thing…if life is going to keep raining on my picnic and I never learn how to use an umbrella, then I don't deserve grilled hot dogs, much less four-layer chocolate cake.

I jump out of my skin when my phone rings. It's Janice, and I sit down, limp with nerves, elated and scared at the same time.

"Maggie, I love what you've done so far, but it's still not quite there."

I think I'm going to die. Instead I open my metaphorical umbrella and listen to this little rain shower with an open mind, really listen.

When she asks, "Do you want to give this project another try?" I tell her yes, because here's the thing: I trust her and I'm learning to trust *me* again.

I'm just punching the off button when Mama comes into the laundry room.

"Your workshop ad is in the paper today. I think I'll go with you tomorrow. I'm tired of being cooped up in this house."

"The workshop's all day. Are you sure you're up to it?"

Mama coughs, not hard and hoarse in the way of a person who has a cold, but in a light, shallow, almost delicate way of a person with a fading heart. I'm torn between hovering over her, watching her breathe, saying, *Conserve your strength* and dragging out her red shoes, watching her dance, saying, *Live it up, life is short.*

"Flitter, I'll be fine. I'll take my pillow and my crossword puzzle and you won't even know I'm there."

* * *

My writing seminar is at Beth Ann's Books and Stuff, and Beth Ann Hanley is the major reason I don't argue with Mama about going with me. Her shop has cozy chairs in every nook and cranny, and she's added hand-crocheted afghans to make sure her customers don't get a chill while they sit and read a first chapter to see if they want to buy. If you decide to read two or three, she'll bring you tea, hot orange spice in winter and iced mint in summer.

She'll treat Mama like an honored guest, and if she gets tired, Beth Ann will take her into the office and plump up the pillows so she can lie down on a yellow-and-blue-flowered chintz sofa.

She and I were roommates at the "W," and ours is the kind of friendship that allows the freedom of absence. Sometimes weeks or even months will go by without us talking, but we always pick up exactly where we left off.

Her shop is on Main Street in Tupelo in a 1940s building with stained-glass windows along the front. Inside are original embossed tin ceiling tiles, ancient wooden floors that smell of lemon wax and ceiling fans with brass-edged wooden paddles that stir the scent of rose and lavender candles. I could live in this bookstore. I'd light different scented candles each day, and start my mornings with a cup of foamy cappuccino from Beth Ann's coffee bar. Then I'd select an armful of books and disappear into an enchanted place of words and other worlds, not my own.

For now, though, I have to stay in this one, upright and steady, smiling as Beth Ann sweeps toward me wearing a purple-and-gold caftan Mama says makes her look too big, and I think makes her look like the goddess of a small, ultra-elegant culture.

She hugs both of us, and Mama thanks her for the spectacular long-stem roses she sent to the hospital.

"You're worth it, Victoria," Beth Ann says.

"I sure am," Mama agrees. "Tell everybody you know."

When she clumps off with her walker to check out Beth Ann's latest selection of crossword-puzzle books, I ask the question that's turning my stomach to knots.

"How many registered?"

I'm hoping for twenty. Fifteen, at the very least. Enough to fill the small bistro tables in the café at the back of Beth Ann's store. Enough to create a lively give-and-take between teacher and student. Enough to make me say to myself, *See, I'm still a writer, people want to hear what I have to say, they want to know what I know—the secret to being somebody with your name on a book cover.*

"Four," she says, and I try to keep from showing my dismay.

Beth Ann sees it anyway. Good friends always do. When she squeezes my hand, I feel better because here is something else best friends do—communicate comfort with touch. No words, no platitudes, just one simple, compassionate touch.

"Well…" I fortify myself with a deep breath and a smile. "Let's set up before the mad rush begins."

I follow Beth Ann to the small back-corner café where she's put a single pink rose in blue crystal vases on each table along with purple pens and small spiral-bound notebooks.

"And you can sit here," she says, leading the way to a wooden rocking chair with a contoured bottom just right for sitting, curved arms perfect for resting my elbows, and delicate, carved roses I can nestle in the palm of my hand if I need to hold on to something beautiful. And I do.

I sink into the rocking chair and set it in motion, close my eyes and lean my head against its tall carved back, wrap my hands around the roses and hang on. Then I hear music—the haunting, bluesy notes of "Wonderful Tonight" as only Eric Clapton can play them, and it takes me a moment to realize the song is coming from Beth Ann's speakers and not my dreams.

"Rainman Jones made that."

"What?"

"The chair you're sitting in. It was carved by WTUP's famous DJ."

"Oh…" Suddenly the chair is electrified, pulsing with some strange kind of energy that could drive you crazy if you'd let it.

Of course, I don't plan to. A DJ who is good with his hands is the last thing I need. Or maybe the first, but lord, lord, who has time to think about that?

"This summer I added some of his smaller carved furniture in the Stuff section. It's selling well."

I don't respond because all I can think of is the mellifluous voice on the radio that has been my safe haven since my *Titanic*-inspired birthday and the butter-slick lips that planted a kiss in my palm. Fortunately the staccato tapping of Mama's metal walker breaks the spell.

"When's the crowd coming?" She sinks into another rocking chair, blue padded seat and no roses, obviously not made by hand.

"Brace yourself, Mama. There are only four."

"Well, flitter, don't they know what they're missing?"

Obviously not. By the time we break for lunch, I'm ready to skewer myself on a brass letter opener. Here's what I expected: the next Stephen King, an Emily Dickinson in the making and a couple of Robert-and-Elizabeth-Barrett-Browning clones.

I got a horror story, all right—a know-it-all dressed in black who interrupted everything I said with a contradictory statement about what he'd read and what he'd heard. And instead of Emily, I got a Sylvia Plath who has spent the last two hours crying and who shouldn't be let near arsenic and speeding trains.

Did I wish for famous lovers? I got them, but I doubt they'll ever go down in history unless her husband discovers the Romeo with leather jeans and Mohawk hair who has spent the entire workshop kissing his wife. I can see the headlines: Murder in Mystery Writer's Workshop.

The only intelligent observation made this entire morning was by Mama when she told the self-appointed oracle, "If you'll just shut up and listen, you might learn something."

"Mama, that wasn't polite," I tell her after my students have scattered for lunch.

"Somebody had to teach him some manners. I can tolerate ugly, but I can't abide rude."

"He wasn't ugly."

"Yes, he was. Anybody with nose hairs and ripped up jeans is ugly in my book. Let's eat. I'm hungry."

Food is the last thing on my mind. I've just netted fifty dollars and six cents. Barely enough for a tank of gas.

If I think about that I won't be able to get through the rest of my workshop, let alone the rest of the week, the rest of my life. What I do is lead Mama to the table where Beth Ann has served three plates of chicken salad. I pick up my fork and concentrate on putting one pecan, one grape and one tiny chunk of mayonnaise-and-sour-cream-encrusted chicken into my mouth. I chew and don't think of anything else except the burst of flavor on my tongue. I will enjoy this moment, this day, having lunch with my dear friend and my irascible mama.

Mama seizes the stage and cracks up everybody with a story about losing her hairpiece in the middle of a fast fox trot at the Rainbow Room in Memphis.

There is a quiet place inside us where angels are whispering, and they're saying, *See?* What I believe they mean is that we are to live boldly and fully, trusting the Universe to take care of the rest. I watch and listen with a heart full of thankfulness.

CHAPTER 13

Today has been one of the hottest on record. If you think July is hot as it gets, hang on to your hat, folks. August promises to be even worse.
—*Rainman*

Sometimes I wonder if Rainman is talking about the weather or my life. I'd probably ask him, but Mama's asleep on her side of the Jeep, and I have bigger things on my mind than having a philosophical discussion with the radio.

With the workshop finally over, I'm headed back to the farm in the midst of one of the most spectacular sunsets I've seen in a long time. Or perhaps they've all been that gorgeous and I'm just now noticing.

I veer off Highway 178 onto back country roads where the colors of the sky are bleeding into the tops of massive oaks, painting lakes and white-fenced pastures and placid cows with red and purple and gold. The angels are applauding and saying, *Live, Maggie, live*.

Well...I thought that's what I'd been doing all along, but I see now that I've simply been making time. Waiting for Mama to bounce back and take over.

It's time to seize control and take center stage of my own life. Be like Mama. Maybe not with red feathers and a desire for a blond wig, but charge ahead, nonetheless.

Mama stirs and looks out the window. "Where are we?"

"We're taking the long way home."

"Good. I wish we wouldn't stop till we got to New York."

"I don't think we can even get there from Plantersville, Mama."

"You can do anything you set your mind to, Maggie."

Mama doesn't make offhand remarks, throwaway statements. There's a whole lecture in those ten words, and I should pay attention.

She sits up straighter and adjusts her glasses. "Do you see that, Maggie? It looks like a Canadian goose."

"Some of them find a friendly pond and stay here year 'round, I think."

"If you and Jean don't quit wrapping me in goose down, I'm going to smother to death. I want to fly."

It's too dark to see, but I can picture that sly look on Mama's face, the one that says, *Pay attention now, hear what I say.* And as I listen, I feel the slow, steady unfurling of wings.

The Wednesday after my workshop is a rare one—no doctors' appointments for Mama or Jean and no crises, large or small. I call Jean to sit with Mama while I take my laptop to the hayloft, a beautiful setting to write, high above the farm with a panoramic view of lush grass, tall trees and cool blue streams.

I wear a yellow sundress. It's a happy, hopeful color that reminds me of the story Aunt Mary Quana tells about her wedding. "Victoria tried to talk me out of wearing yellow, told me virgins always wear white, and I said, 'I'm not planning on being one for long, so you might as well shut up.'"

Reveling in my freedom, I lie in the sweet clover hay, close my eyes and spread my arms like angel wings. Then, kissed by sunshine and my muse, I open the laptop and fall into my unicorn story, writing straight through lunch and into the early afternoon.

My cell phone startles me back to the real world.

"Maggie. I'm at Baskin-Robbins." This thrills me,

just the way Joe says my name, the way ice cream makes him think of me. "Where are you?"

When I tell him, he says, "How about a banana split? Delivered."

It's just ice cream, I tell myself while I wait for him. But when he climbs the ladder and digs into a mound of vanilla topped by whipped cream and a cherry twenty minutes later, I'm vividly aware of his mouth… and the glorious things a sensitive, caring man like Rainman can do with it.

He makes me feel sixteen. Correct that. Sixteen with the mature sensibilities of a woman ready to explore the many ways you can fly to the moon.

For now, though, eating ice cream will do.

"I love lazy afternoons like this," he says.

"Ice cream and good company always make them better."

"One of these days, Maggie, I'm going to ask you for a real date."

"One of these days, I might say yes."

He leans over to pluck a strand of hay from my hair, and then kisses the springy curl that wraps around his finger.

"I have to get back to the station. Take care of yourself, pretty lady."

Amazing, the power of one small gesture, the beauty

of tender caring. Joe makes me believe that all things are possible, even this—a man and a woman transcending obstacles to reach for something magical.

I'm still dreaming of possibilities as I drive to Dr. Holman's office on Thursday for Mama's checkup.

He listens to her heart and her lungs, checks her eyes, her ears and her swollen feet, while I sit on a hard plastic chair and try to map out a different life for myself.

Maybe I could date Joe, after all. Maybe everything doesn't have to be perfect to reach for magic.

While the nurses help Mama dress, Dr. Holman calls me into his office. Not a good sign.

"The increased swelling in her feet and the dry cough are indicators that her heart continues to fail. Maggie, it's time to consider a personal-care home."

I feel as if clouds have gathered over my head and turned loose a monsoon and I'm caught without an umbrella. Mama will never stand for such a move, and I don't know if Jean and I could survive it.

"How long before I have to make this decision?"

"A few weeks, Maggie. A couple of months at most."

Change has a way of throwing you off balance, flipping you upside down so you don't know which way to turn, and I'm reeling from this turn of events.

When I get home, maybe I'll take a bubble bath, see if I can soak out the misery and think up a solution. That is, if I can carve out some time for myself.

Instead of scented bubbles, what I get is total immersion in the funeral plans of three feisty septuagenarians. Laura Kate Lindsey and Annie Maycomb have come to visit in Laura Kate's ancient brown Chevrolet Impala.

I try to tune out this conversation, especially in light of Dr. Holman's prognosis, but Mama drags me right in. "Maggie, if you let Lula Bell Franks caterwaul 'Whispering Hope' at my funeral, I'm going to kill you."

Before I can make a premature deathbed promise, Annie Maycomb says, "My grandkids are going to sing at mine."

She's bragging, and I watch Mama snatch the limelight.

"Well, *my* daughters are going to hire a brass band. Take notes, Maggie." She makes sure to catch my eye, letting me know she means business. "I'm planning to go out in style while they play 'When the Saints Go Marching In.'"

"You're no saint, Victoria," Laura Kate says.

"Anybody who's going to have her ashes scattered

at Wal-Mart to make sure her daughter will visit has no business talking about my religion."

"When Sylvia Liscomb died," Annie says, "her sorry daughter left her ashes in the back seat of her Buick for a year…in a McRae's shopping bag."

"Lord, lord," Laura Kate says. "What if somebody had stolen the car and carried it off to Mexico? Poor old Sylvia couldn't even speak Spanish."

"What difference does it make? She was dead," Mama says, irritated. "You two just hush up and listen. I'm not through planning my funeral."

Does she know what her doctor said? I wouldn't put it past her to have sneaked down the hall and listened at the door.

When Mama walks Laura Kate and Annie out, I notice that her feet have swollen over the tops of her shoes. At dinner I make sure she takes her fluid pill, as she calls it, and then I watch every bird bite she takes, measuring each spoonful in terms of calories and nutrition.

Finally I help her into bed, and she catches my hand. "I wasn't kidding about the music."

"Hush, Mama. You're not dying."

"I'm not going to live forever, Maggie. I want them to play 'How Great Thou Art,' too."

I can't stand this. Not without Jean. Not without…

somebody. And so I do what all the Lucases do in times of crisis.

"That's appropriate, Mama. Everybody will know the song is talking about you."

"They'd better." She flounces over and turns her back to me, but not before I see what I'm looking for. Mama's eyes may be fading, as blue ones are prone to do, but there's still a light inside, a bit of devilment that says, *I'm not done here, yet, and don't you forget it.*

After I hear Mama's snores, I call to tell Jean the latest news.

"Maggie, what are we going to do?"

"Pray," I reply, and then I light a white candle and go outside to sit on the front porch swing. I wish I were Catholic so I could hang on to a rosary while I say Hail Marys. Instead I look up at the silver moon and say please.

CHAPTER 14

It's great weather for watching tonight's full eclipse of the moon. These eclipses usually shake things up, so expect some seismic shifts, folks.
—*Rainman*

"Let's stay up late and watch the eclipse, Maggie."

We're on the way to Woody's Restaurant to meet Jean and Walter, who just got home yesterday. Mama's in the passenger seat with a pillow behind her back, a lap robe over her knees because she says the car's air conditioner freezes her to death, and her walker folded in the back seat. Trappings of her future.

And mine. Unless Rainman's moon brings a few seismic shifts my way.

"We will, Mama," I say. But my mind's not on watching the heavens, or the big announcement Walter and Jean plan to make. It's on Mama's long-term health care.

"We want tonight to be a huge occasion for Mama," my sister told me on the phone this afternoon. "Make sure she's dressed up."

As if I have to. Mama's partial to pearls and sequins, and rarely gets into the car without them. Tonight she's in a red pantsuit with jewel-encrusted lapels. If it weren't for her new, extrawide, rubber-soled, flat-heeled shoes, you'd think she was going dancing.

Walter has reserved a private room and filled it with pink roses and pink candles. When we walk in, Mama says, "Whose birthday is it? Mine?"

They all laugh, Mama loudest of all, but I'm remembering her saying this morning, while sitting in bed with her nightcap askew, "Maggie, quick, get the paper so I can see the date. I don't remember if this is July or August."

"Friday, July twenty-eighth," I told her, and then because she looked so distressed, I said, "It's all right. Everybody forgets sometimes."

Now Jean says, "It's a different kind of celebration, Mama. Walter and I are going to have a baby."

"Honey, I thought we were going to wait till everybody had ordered," Walter replies.

"Maggie, quick, call Annie Maycomb," Mama says. "Her grandkids might as well move over because my grandbaby's going to be the president of the United States."

She does a little hula, impatient that her walker confines her movements, while I refold my napkin and try to figure out the future.

"Maggie," she continues, "I want you to tell everybody in church Sunday."

"We'll have an announcement put in the bulletin," Jean adds.

"Flitter. Nobody reads those old things. I want Maggie to announce it from the pulpit."

So now I'm trying to figure out how I'll manage that, because if I don't, Mama will.

The waitress is hovering over her now. "I want the most expensive thing on the menu," Mama says. "It's not every day a woman discovers she's going to have the smartest grandbaby in the world."

After dinner, while Walter helps Mama into the car, Jean tugs me into the foyer and says, "You were awfully quiet tonight. What's wrong?"

"I'm thinking about my future, Jean. I have to find some kind of work to tide me over until I'm back on a career path."

"I know you do. But I'm not fixing to be a party to

putting Mama in one of those awful homes. Besides, what would we do without her?"

"We wouldn't be without her. She'd just be in a different place, that's all." Why do I feel like a villain here? "I don't think they're all awful, either."

"Well, she does, and I can't think of any other options because you know she's not going to tolerate a stranger living in her house."

"I know."

"What are we going to do, Maggie?"

Who made me Solomon? I want to say. Instead I hand my sister a tissue.

"What we're not going to do is cry in the foyer of a fancy restaurant."

I hurry to the car because Walter's heading our way, and if I don't show up behind the wheel of the Jeep within the next three seconds, Mama will be honking the horn.

As soon as we get home, I help Mama to bed, sans walker. Leaning heavily on me, she stumbles. I brace myself, amazed that somebody who has lost as much weight as she can deliver a linebacker blow. Frantically I grab for the back of her recliner for extra support. We teeter there, and in that split second I'm trying to figure how I'll cushion Mama's fall when we hit the floor.

She grabs the chair, too, and with Herculean effort we both remain upright. Finally, we move forward again, and when I get her into bed she lies for a while, silent.

"Are you okay, Mama?"

"Wake me up for the eclipse," is all she says, and then shuts her eyes.

I stand for a moment, watching, but she peers at me with one eye, and says, "Go on, Maggie. I can't sleep with you staring at me."

I tiptoe out, then hole up in my bedroom with the telephone book and my laptop. It takes a while before I'm calm enough to start making a list of the area's high schools.

Life goes on, I tell myself, and finally I begin typing. First thing Monday morning, I'll call everybody on my list to see if there's an opening for an English teacher.

There's a certain satisfaction in thinking of myself back in the classroom, molding young minds, inspiring young writers, dispensing motherly love along with lessons about subject-verb agreement and the correct use of pronouns.

I don't see this job as a replacement for writing, never that, but a steady income that would remove a huge pressure and allow me to write with wings.

Jefferson noses open my door and pads across the

carpet to put his big head in my lap. This is his way of checking on his family, making sure that all of us are in the proper place at the proper time. I smooth his re-growing fur. "It's okay, boy. I'll go to bed eventually."

He whines softly, understanding more than most people give dogs credit for. If you'd lived ten years with somebody who spoke a different language, wouldn't you at least learn to understand what they're saying?

"I'm making plans," I tell him, "but I don't want you to worry and lose your hair. I'm going to make sure that you and Mama are taken care of. Okay, boy?"

He nudges my arm, which means I should continue patting, then pads back to Mama's bedroom.

I wake Mama at midnight, and she says, "What's wrong? Is the baby sick?"

"Mama, Jean hasn't had her baby. It's the eclipse. Remember?"

"Certainly, I do," she snaps. "I was dreaming, that's all."

I help her get into a robe and house shoes, then make sure she's anchored solidly to her walker before I take her onto the front porch.

The earth's shadow has already started its march across the moon. I position two wicker chairs exactly right for viewing, and we turn our faces toward the heavens.

"This is the most spectacular one yet," Mama says, and I agree.

Only a tiny sliver of gold shows where the rim of the moon is still not blotted out. When complete darkness comes, I am filled with awe and wonder and a sense of my own mortality. *This will endure.* There's a kind of mercy in that thought, in the knowledge that I'm merely passing through, and no matter what I do, no matter what kind of legacy I leave, I can never match this; I can never create a star or call forth a storm or cause a total eclipse of the moon.

It's beautiful, this kind of hushed watching, the two of us with our faces lifted and the fragrance of Mama's Gertrude Jekyll rose heavy on the summer air. The earth's shadow continues its journey, leaving behind a moon that glows red.

"Maggie." Without taking her eyes off the transformed moon, Mama reaches for my hand. "I'm leaving."

"Don't talk that way. You're not going anywhere."

"Flitter, I'm not talking about dying. I'm talking about going into a home like Mary Quana." She glances at me and adds, "Just till I can get back on my feet. If she can have fun in one of those things, so can I."

My squeezed-tight throat blocks words and, when I don't say anything, she treats me to one of her famous sly looks. "Besides, I'm tired of being the Statue of Liberty for you and Jean. It's high time both of you get on with your own lives."

Mama didn't say a word about need—hers to have a nurse standing by and mine to get a job and a life. She didn't mention the kind of courage it takes to chart a new course, or the heartache of wrenching herself away from a place she loves. She's always been one to plow forward and never look back with regret.

Mercy, I think as I look at the red moon. A mercy that I found hard to ask for and Mama found easy to grant.

The next morning, I hear her on the phone at six o'clock. "Get up and get dressed, Jean," she's saying. "We're going to look at personal-care homes."

I go into her bedroom with uncombed hair and bleary, bloodshot eyes. Mama's sitting in her recliner already dressed in blue pedal pushers and matching blue blouse that sports a green-sequined parrot on the shoulder.

How did she do all that without waking me? A scary thought.

"Mama...what on earth? Do you know what time it is?"

"Certainly. I'm not senile."

"Nobody said you were. All I'm saying is that none of these places will be open for hours. Besides, we don't have to look today. Walter just got home."

"Walter can wait. I need to get settled in. Go on and get dressed. We'll eat breakfast at Shoney's."

By seven o'clock we're in my Jeep headed to Shoney's breakfast buffet, Mama up front on her stack of pillows and Jean in the back seat in her brand-new pink maternity top she couldn't wait to start wearing, a pen in her hand and the telephone book plus a loose-leaf notebook open on her lap.

"I've made a list of all the places we should visit," she says. "And I'm making a list of all the things we should look for."

"A courteous, kind-hearted staff is the main thing," I say.

"It's got to be clean first," Jean adds. "We don't want carpet that smells like urine."

"We've got to find one with a good nurse on duty."

"Obviously, Maggie, but what I'm worried about is finding one that doesn't invite all those hellfire-and-damnation preachers who come in and scream at everybody. Mama won't put up with that."

"We can't control the programs, Jean. Besides, I think attendance is optional."

"You'd better ask. And while you're at it, see about the laundry. They mix up your clothes, and what they don't lose they bleach to pieces."

Am I the only one with a mouth? I want to say, but if I do, Jean will start crying and I'm all out of tissues.

"Nobody asked me what I wanted," Mama says.

We both ask, "What?"

"I'm looking for one that has a good-looking old geezer with all his own teeth and at least half his mind."

"Mama, this is serious," Jean says. "Quit joking."

"Who said I'm joking?"

With Mama you never know. The good thing is that at least I don't have to worry about having a baby brother or sister.

"I'd also like one that takes dogs," Mama says, and I tell her that's the first thing I'll ask.

At Shoney's it takes both of us to get Mama out of the car and onto her walker. Jean tears up, and I give her a don't-you-dare look. I won't have Mama's Declaration of Independence day marred with tears.

What I think about, though, is how close she came to falling last night and how helpless I felt to prevent it. At least, in a home, professionals will be there to take care of her.

Inside I load my plate with one of everything at the food bar, and so does Jean. "I'm eating for two," she says. I could tell her I'm eating for depression, but I don't.

Instead I tell Mama to take another helping of cheese grits. "I might as well," she says. "If I'm going to find a man, I've got to get my figure back."

The first place we visit is Summer Valley, a lovely name that conjures images of sunlight pouring through French windows onto butter-yellow walls, wrought-iron gliders tucked among arbors laden with soft pink New Dawn roses, and a light-filled dining room where the food is so delicious you think you're eating at Antoine's in New Orleans.

What we discover is a rectangular brick building with windows so high that nobody can possibly see the view. They wouldn't want to if they could because the yard sports nut grass and a few bitterweeds interspersed with brown-earth patches where army worms have eaten all the grass.

"I'm not getting out," Jean says. "Let's go."

I agree with her. This place looks as if it should house prisoners instead of senior citizens who were once our teachers and doctors and lawyers and tax accountants, people with lively minds and humorous outlooks. Even if illness has stolen their minds, they deserve graciousness and beauty.

"Mama?" I turn to her for the last word.

"I guess it won't hurt to see," she tells me, but I'm reading her face. *Help*.

I accelerate and turn around, but the driveway is too narrow and I end up backing onto the lawn and crushing some crabgrass. An improvement, I'd say.

"There are plenty of other places," I tell Mama.

"If not, we can come back," she replies. "This is only temporary."

All day Jean and I both act as if we believe that, but awful truths have a way of creeping up on you in the dark. With Mama and Jefferson both snoring, I'm standing in the kitchen doing dishes, with nothing but the radio to keep me company.

"Expect some bad weather tomorrow," Rainman says. "It's already here."

Suddenly the terrible loneliness of having no one to share heartache is unbearable. Even triumph and celebration are better with somebody special.

With a bluesy rendition of "Stormy Weather" playing, I dial Rainman's number. "Hello, this is Maggie." And then I stop. Just stop.

"Maggie? Where are you? What's wrong?"

When I'm blue, my flattened-out voice is a dead giveaway to my friends. Knowing he hears the pain gives me courage.

I tell him about Mama and the dreadful search, and when I'm done he says, "I would come if I weren't at the station, but I have a song I'm going to play for you, Maggie. Hang on… I'll be right back."

I do just what he says, hang on while "Stormy Weather" ends, and Rainman comes back on the air. "This next song is for someone very special," he says, and something inside me relaxes.

"I discovered this singer at a time in my life when I needed reassurance and grace, and nobody delivers it better than Price Harris…. Here he is, folks. 'I've Never Been Out of His Care.'"

While a rich, mellow voice assures me that the arms of God are around me, I feel as if I've been hugged.

Rainman comes back on the phone. "Talk to me, Maggie. I'm here all night if you need me."

"I do," I tell him, and then sweet release comes, tears and the comfort of talking to someone with the wisdom to let me cry.

CHAPTER 15

It's a gloomy Monday, folks. If you're going anywhere, carry an umbrella, because those dark
clouds are brewing up a summer storm.
—*Rainman*

The next morning, I hole up in my bedroom making
phone calls to the area's schools and hoping the storm
front will pass. If Jean and I don't find a decent place
for Mama, I might as well forget second career and cash
flow.

In the two hours I spend on the phone, I get six
sorrys and one "You're too late. Don't you know we fill
our teaching positions in the spring?"

How do you respond to that? *No, I'm so dumb I
thought everybody waited till the last minute? Yes, I know
but I just wanted to see how rude you'd act if I tried?*

"How did it go?" Jean and Mama want to know when I emerge.

"Let me fix some tea first. Do we have any Jack Daniel's in the house?"

Jean says, "Call them back and tell them you have to have a job."

"Maggie's too good for a small-town high school," Mama argues. "She needs to be at a major university where they'll appreciate her."

"You can talk to me, Mama. I'm in this room."

"I *was* talking to you, Miss Priss."

"If you'll recall, I don't have a Ph.D."

"Flitter, a Ph.D. doesn't amount to a fart in a whirlwind compared to your accomplishments. Go fix me some tea. And add lots of sugar. We've got to hunt for a good place for me to hang my hat for a little while."

"We can wait till tomorrow, Mama."

"No. I'm going today."

Fortunately the thunderstorm passes, but it's still drizzling. I'm bundling Mama into raincoat and boots when the doorbell rings.

"I'll get that," Jean says. She comes back with an armful of stargazer lilies, their pink throats damp with moisture and their sweet perfume filling the room.

"Who's sending me flowers?" Mama says.

"They're for Maggie."

Oh… I'm so excited I drop the card, but I don't need to see the name. I know. I *know*.

Maggie, it reads. *These lilies remind me of you. Keep your chin up and your eyes on the stars. Joe.*

Unexpected beauty and tenderness always make me cry.

"Who sent them?" Jean says, and I tell her. "Why?"

"None of your business, Jean," Mama snaps. "He's cute, Maggie. If he sent flowers to me, I wouldn't cry. I'd call him back and invite him to dinner."

"Maybe I will, Mama. But first, we have things to do."

There's only one personal-care home we haven't seen in this area. *Please, please,* I pray as I drive because I'm not willing to put Mama in a place fifty or sixty miles from home. Both Jean and I want her close enough so that she can call and say come, and we can be there in fifteen minutes.

We're skirting Tupelo on the 45 bypass, heading to a place five minutes south of the city. It's called Belle Gardens, but I'm too smart to let a lovely name fool me again.

"I just have a feeling about this one," Mama declares.

"Good or bad?"

Before she can answer, Jean says, "If they don't offer private visiting rooms so the family won't have to sit in one of those awful reception rooms that looks like a bowling alley, I'm voting against it."

"Who says you get a vote? I'm the one staying, not you."

"But, Mama, we don't want you to have to sit around in a place full of people in wheelchairs."

"Nothing wrong with that. I'm planning to get one myself, soon. Electric. With designer hubcaps and a souped-up engine. I might even fly the rebel flag off the back."

Oh… My heart hurts. I'm going to miss Mama's tart tongue and sassy mouth. Maybe I'll ask if they have a room for two and move in with her.

Jean's sniffling, and Mama orders, "Perk up. After we look at Belle Gardens I want to go shopping for baby stuff. I want to pick out the nursery furniture. Oh…and the coming-home-from-the-hospital outfit and the christening gown."

"Are you going to leave anything for me and Walter, Mama?"

"I don't plan on it."

Belle Gardens rises out of the mists, a gracious white-columned mansion with a circular driveway sweeping around a two-acre lot. There are trees here—

ancient magnolias and massive black jack oaks shading a walking track and a wide front porch—and masses of roses with the tended look of a garden cared for by somebody in a wide-brimmed summer hat and white cotton gloves.

I park in the shade and hold my breath as we walk through the front door. Sunlight streams through French windows and bookshelves line the walls. In the corner, a woman with white curls and red fingernail polish is sitting at an upright piano playing "Tennessee Waltz."

At last I can breathe. And as the air slowly expands my lungs, it feels as if I haven't breathed in a very long time.

On Saturday, Mama moves to Belle Gardens amid laughter (hers), tears (Jean's) and lots of huffing and puffing (mine and Walter's). Only two things mar this move: dogs aren't allowed and a private room won't be available until the fifteenth of August.

"Two weeks won't kill me," Mama says. After we've hung her clothes and put her family photographs on her side of the double dresser, she says, "Maggie, take care of Jefferson till I get back home."

Her roommate, Carolyn West, watches from her rocking chair in the corner by the window. "Nobody leaves this place," she remarks, and I want to strangle her.

Instead, Jean and I settle onto Mama's bed and glare at Carolyn while Mama arranges her lap robe over her recliner.

"I'll just head for home," Walter says. "Take your time, honey."

He kisses Jean and leaves us in this bare-walled room with a stranger who will be sleeping next to Mama at night, listening to her breathe.

If Mama has a heart attack, will this woman punch the call button? Will she hog the bathroom? Turn the light off while Mama's still working crossword puzzles?

Now is the big moment, leaving Mama behind. Suddenly I don't know what to say.

"Well…" Jean begins, and for once even Mama is speechless.

I crumple the bedspread between my fingers, then smooth it out again. The faucet in the bathroom is dripping—Niagara Falls—and I get up and twist the handles back. Hard. I've stopped the drip, but I can't go back into the bedroom just yet. Instead I anchor myself to the cool porcelain sink and hang on.

Okay, I say to myself. *Okay. What next?*

I thought I was doing great. Making a list of

changes and marking them off. First a job search and then Mama.

How awful is that? Marking off your own mama? I look at my flushed face in the mirror, my sweat-frizzed hair. Well…I didn't actually mark her off.

Did I?

This is insane. How can I feel guilty about finding a beautiful place where Mama will receive the best of care, where she can settle in and be happy while I work?

Where? So far, nobody's interested in my résumé.

"Maggie?"

"Coming, Mama."

She looks so fragile sitting in that big chair that I want to scoop her up and carry her home, fold her in her white fuzzy blanket and sit by the bed, holding her hand.

"It's time for supper."

"We'll take you out, Mama. To Harvey's. You like their shrimp."

"No, I want to meet everybody."

"You're sure? We can bring you back after dinner."

"You and Jean go on. I've got to put on some lipstick. I plan to knock their socks off."

Our footsteps echo on the tiled hallway of Belle Gardens. I can't bear to look back, can't endure the thought of seeing Mama standing in her doorway on her walker. Brave and alone.

The Jeep is blazing hot in spite of the shade, and I crank up the air conditioner. We sit there with it blowing our faces, not speaking, not daring.

Finally I say, "Are you ready to go home?"

"Not yet. Let's go somewhere, get a drink. Then we can come back and check on Mama."

I nod and don't even ask where. It doesn't matter. What matters is marking time.

We go to Harvey's and sit in a corner booth, me with a big strawberry daiquiri and Jean with a safe strawberry milkshake.

"This is horrible," she says, and I know she's not talking about the drink.

"It's life," I reply.

"Well, it's shitty."

"Yes." I lift my glass and feel the cool iced liquor slide down my throat. "But not always."

"That's what Aunt Mary Quana said."

"You told her about Belle Gardens?"

"Yes. She'd be mad as a wet hen if I hadn't." Jean unrolls the big linen napkin, dumps the silver and blows her nose. "Can we go back now?"

"It's too soon. Let's give her time to finish dinner."

"We'll take her back home if she hates it."

"Absolutely."

While Jean toys with her milkshake, I sip my drink, miserable, second-guessing myself, wondering if I could have found a better solution.

"I have Walter…and the baby. What are you going to do, Maggie?"

"Take care of Jefferson and Mama's house and… I don't know."

"Walter has contacts. He can get you a job."

How do I say I *have to do this alone* and make my sister understand? I don't want merely a job. I want a future, one I've discovered, created, worked for, carved out and earned. Not one that has been handed to me by somebody with power.

"Thank you," I finally tell my sister. "If nothing else works out, I'll let you know."

"He's leaving tomorrow. For London. I could kill him."

"It's his job, Jean."

"Well, if he doesn't change so he can stay home with me and the baby, I'm going to divorce him."

"You wouldn't."

"I would. Every baby deserves two parents, and if Walter's not willing to be the other one, then I'll find somebody who will."

"You sound like Mama. I didn't know you had it in you."

"I didn't either until just now." She reaches for my hand. "And so do you, Maggie. You're going to get out there and wow somebody."

Do women my age get to have two great careers in a lifetime? Two good men? Is there a god of second chances?

The waitress comes and we pay for our drinks. Then I link arms with my sister and say, "Do you know something? You ought to be in charge of the world."

"Really?"

"Yes, really. Let's go check on Mama."

The sun is down and the Jeep is cooler when we climb in this time. I wait through two lights behind the Saturday-night-dinner crowd, and then head south on Gloster Street.

"Oh, lord," Jean says. "Wait."

"What?" I'm thinking she's having a miscarriage, and it takes a strong will not to slam on the brakes and cause a six-car pileup.

"I've got a Harvey's napkin in my purse. We've got to go back."

"You nearly gave me a heart attack." I keep on driving south. "We'll drop it off the next time we're there."

"What if they miss it and send the cops? I don't want my baby to have a jailbird mother."

"Good grief, Jean."

"Well, I don't."

I turn around and go back to Harvey's, not because I'm afraid Jean will go to jail, but because we put our mama into a place that locks the front doors after eleven at night so nobody can get in. Not even family.

Finally we make it back to Belle Gardens, and Jean and I reach for each other's hands before we walk inside.

The first thing we hear is laughter. Mama's.

She's sitting on the faux-velvet sofa between two women—one amply padded and lively faced, the other petite and spry-looking with a face as brown and wrinkled as a peach pit. And in a chair opposite sits Aunt Mary Quana, her hair the vivid color of a redbird.

Mama waves us over. "Look who just breezed in from Atlanta. And I want you to meet my new friends, Mert and Sarah."

We say hello, and then Aunt Mary Quana, who always jumps straight to the point, says, "How do you like my hair? Don't you think it looks natural?" Forget explanations about when she got here and how long she's going to stay. "I'm going to quit coloring it when I'm a hundred. That gives me forty more years."

"It does not," Mama argues. "It gives you thirty, because I'm only five years older than you and I'm seventy-five."

"How can I lie about my age if you won't? Just speak for yourself, Victoria."

"I didn't see your car, Aunt Mary Quana," I say.

"That's because I didn't want you to. I'm parked out back in the overnight-guest lot. You didn't think I'd let Victoria have all the fun without me, did you?"

We stay until the day shift leaves and the night shift starts locking the doors.

On the way home, Jean comments, "I didn't know they'd let you push rollaway cots into rooms. We should have stayed, too."

"Hush, Jean. Just be grateful."

Cocooned in darkness, the tires of the Jeep swishing against pavement damp from a late-afternoon rain, I remember Mama laughing, and suddenly everything seems possible.

CHAPTER 16

These are the last dog days of summer, but fall is just around the corner. If you're driving, don't let the heat get to you. Road rage is a dangerous thing.

—*Rainman*

I feel guilty waking up in Mama's house with nobody to tend to except the dog. It has been so long since I've had time to myself that I can't think what to do first. Job hunt? Work on my unicorn fantasy? Work on revisions for my mystery? Cook breakfast? Eat cake?

Why not? A woman whose whole house smells like stargazer lilies deserves cake for breakfast. Maybe I'll sit on a silk cushion to eat it.

I go into the kitchen, turn on the radio and start making a four-layer, double-chocolate cake, my specialty. Jefferson thumps his tail, expecting a bite, but I give him a doggy treat instead.

"No chocolate for you, boy. It'll make you sick."

On the radio, Rainman says, "On hot days like this, I enjoy ice cream. Preferably shared."

Is he remembering the hayloft? Is he hoping I'm listening?

The cake turns out better than I'd imagined, perfect, really, and I go outside to pick three lush gardenias, August Beauty, which has a lovely habit of blooming all summer.

I arrange these on top of the cake, put it in a Tupperware carrier, then grab two china plates and two silver forks and head out the door.

In the car I'm almost too giddy to drive. I can't believe I'm doing this, streaking off to WTUP without calling ahead, the woman who has always hated surprises.

Will Joe be there? *Oh*, I hope so.

He *is* there, and he hugs me close and long, even before he notices the cake.

"I brought you something." I lift the lid and the rich aroma of warm chocolate fills the room. "A man who listens to a woman cry and then sends stargazer lilies deserves cake for breakfast."

"Wow! Maggie, I don't know what to say."

"You're not supposed to talk. Just eat."

I wish I could bottle the look he gives me and put it under my pillow. Suddenly this tiny room is fifteen degrees hotter.

"I'm going to enjoy that," he says, and I don't think he's talking about cake.

Breakfast has never been this exciting. After we finish two huge chunks, Joe washes the chocolate off the stems of the gardenias and tucks them in my hair. "You should always wear flowers, Maggie."

The important thing is not wearing the flowers, but having a tender man who gives them to me. Now I understand why my flying-apart sister never completely disintegrates: she has the luxury of tears because Walter is always there to pick up the pieces.

Not that I want to be as dependent as her. Still, I want more than a job and a house with a yard big enough for a dog. I want a *home* with a sweet and tender man who also knows how to make me sizzle. A man like Joe.

"Can you stay, Maggie? I'm off at two."

"I wish I could, Joe, but I have too many things to do. Can I take a rain check?"

"Anytime, Maggie."

He kisses my cheek, and in the car, I sit with my hand over the spot, feeling feminine and hopeful.

* * *

As soon as I get home I write down the things I need to do by priority, and *get a job* tops the list. I'm going to do this or die trying. I haven't depended on a man for financial support yet, and I'm not fixing to start. Mississippi has three major universities within a sixty-mile radius of Mooreville…and another in the southern part of the state. Maybe I'll take Mama's advice and start there. But which one first?

In the midst of my quandary, Jean calls to remind me of her doctor's appointment this afternoon.

Here's another thing…how can I look for a job, much less do one, if I'm always behind the wheel taking my sister somewhere?

"I'm going to teach you how to drive," I tell her.

"Well…all right," she agrees. Have aliens taken over my sister's body, or has pregnancy given her a newfound confidence? If so, maybe I ought to go off and get pregnant. The thought makes me blush because it's not the getting-pregnant part I'm thinking about but the process. With Joe.

"But I'm warning you, Maggie, it will take a while because I'm scared to death, and I'm not fixing to get out onto the highways because I don't want to wreck the car and hurt myself."

"All right, then. We'll practice in Mama's pasture."

"Not today. I'm expecting Walter to call, and I'm laying down the law. He can either arrange to keep his butt at home or find somebody else to keep his baked chicken warm."

"I've never heard it called that."

"You're terrible."

"I know."

After we talk, I close my eyes and point my finger, picking one of the three universities, blind. Mississippi University for Women, commonly known as "the W," is the winner, and before I can change my mind, I pick up the phone and dial.

"English department," I say. "The dean."

I present my credentials for teaching freshman comp and sophomore lit, all the time realizing that this spur-of-the-moment call was not the way to do this. In person, that's the way to get a job. I should have asked this Dean Raskin to set up an interview. Still, I know universities use students working on master's degrees to teach these classes, and I'm infinitely more qualified.

With my fingers crossed behind my back and gardenias wilting in my hair, I wait for him to tell me, "You're a godsend, just what we've been looking for."

Instead I nod and murmur into the telephone that I understand, while he informs me how they already have everybody they need and can't possibly use a

Johnny-come-lately with bushed-out hair and the wrong degree. Of course, he doesn't say that last part, but that's what it feels like.

I stomp down the driveway, check the mailbox hoping for something wonderful, and pull out a flier from Home Depot advertising aluminum siding at fifteen percent off. I rip it to shreds and then storm back to the house and fling the pieces in the garbage can.

It's two hours before Jean's appointment, so I open my computer. But the words are stuck inside me, blocked by wounded pride and the niggling fear that I can't make it on my own. I know better than to force them, and so I take Jefferson and try to reclaim myself on the farmland I love.

After Jean's appointment, we stop by Belle Gardens. Mama is sitting in the library with Aunt Mary Quana, reading, the pockets in the carryall on her walker bulging with tissue, crossword-puzzle books and a box of chocolate-covered cherries.

"I'm fixing to kill my roommate," she says.

"I'll help you," Aunt Mary Quana offers.

"Why?" I'm not alarmed by her declaration. Mama uses this threat on everybody, from the hairstylist she declared made her hair look like a buzzard's butt to her daughter (that would be me) for letting Jefferson lose his hair.

"She can't keep her paws off my candy."

"Well, Mama…share," Jean urges her. "We'll get you some more."

"I gave her one piece. That ought to be enough. But she's a hog."

"*Mama*," I said, and she gives me a sly, wicked grin.

This is just her way of showing us her spirit's intact, that nothing can steal it, not even a strange place filled with the aged and the dying.

Of course, we're all dying. Every day of our lives. But we're living, too. And it's how we do it that counts.

"Jean, I'm driving over to your house tomorrow to stay with you till I get a room here," Aunt Mary Quana says.

"That's wonderful," Jean replies, "moving here to be next to Mama."

"Shoot, I'm not moving here for Victoria. I'm leaving Atlanta because that Jezebel hussy down the hall stole my boyfriend. I'm not fixing to hang around and watch her carry on with Mr. Whitaker."

"What about Uncle Larry?" I ask.

Aunt Mary Quana and her husband were inseparable, both brilliant photojournalists who traveled the world together chasing stories. She still visits his grave once a week, and although she has no children to bind her to Atlanta, I never thought she'd leave Uncle Larry behind.

"I'm not leaving him. I'm fixing to have him exhumed and cremated so I can bring his ashes with me."

"That's morbid," Mama says.

"You won't think so when I put him on my bedside table as inspiration."

"Flitter, I don't need inspiration from Carter. Nor permission, either. I'm getting me a man who's alive."

Let me learn from them, I'm thinking. Let me always plow full speed ahead, no matter what, embracing life with arms wide open.

After we go to Wal-Mart and buy Mama enough chocolates to feed a small independent nation, Jean and I head home in the midst of a sunset that could have been designed by Walt Disney Studios.

"Maggie, when we grow old, do you think we'll be like them?"

"I hope so, Jean. I really do."

It's a good day for traveling, the green of trees and pastureland looking newly minted from last night's shower, the sun warming my driving arm through the window and turning herds of grazing cattle along the roadside into a painting. I'm alone. Nothing but the sound of a moody blues harmonica on the radio and my own blood flowing through my veins to keep me company.

That's the way I want it. I'm passing Belle Gardens now, but I won't stop until the return trip. Mama's probably hiding yesterday's haul of chocolates, and although Jean and I put some in a separate bag for her roommate, I figure Mama handed her one box and gave the rest to Mert and Sarah. Or kept them for herself. With Mama, you never know.

Well, you do, actually. You can always count on her sass and courage, no matter what her circumstances.

And Jean… I'm sure she talked to Walter yesterday, but I don't want to know. I need to be rowing my own boat, and it's a good sign that she didn't call to say *Maggie, what am I going to do?*

What I'm doing is heading south on Highway 45 to Starkville where I will finally do what Mama has said all along. *If you don't toot your own horn, who will?*

At the very least, MSU will offer me a job…teaching creative writing, which is what I should have asked for in the first place. Professional writers aren't lurking behind every camellia bush and magnolia tree in Mississippi, and they'd be darned lucky to have me. I hope I can tell them that with a certain amount of modesty and a whole lot of moxie.

I have plenty of time to get my moxie up because this drive is seventy miles, an hour and fifteen minutes from Mama's front door to the university's entrance, all of it on good four-lane highway after I get out of Mooreville and through the south end of Tupelo. I could get nervous if I think about my bold move—lobbying to be a professor two weeks before the start of fall semester.

Instead I think about traveling on a good road. Is this a metaphor for my life? As Mama would say, *It's high time something good happened.*

I'm taking some of my books with me, *Calico Death*, my first, and *Siamese Silence*, my favorite—both of them in French, German, Italian and Spanish, as well as English.

I had to go to my rented storage unit last night and dig around before I found them. They were piled under boxes labeled Kitchen Stuff and Skinny Clothes I Might Wear Again.

I waded through stacked kitchen chairs, my blue velvet footstool (which I absolutely love and wish I'd taken to Mama's, but where would I put it?), my six-foot desk and swivel office chair, and sixteen boxes of shoes before I could get to the books.

There was something lonely and sad-looking about

my stored possessions, as if I had died and left them behind. And perhaps I have.

No, that's not exactly right. I'm trying to keep the best parts of me. Maybe I'm a cygnet molting its ugly dark feathers so it can become a swan, or a butterfly emerging from its cocoon. Both of them can fly. Yes, I like that, the idea of me lifting my wings to the wind, rising above the mundane and soaring toward the stars.

A trucker in a Peterbilt rig whizzes by, rocking the Jeep, ruffling my wings. Nothing can make me fold them, though. I give him a jaunty wave, but he doesn't wave back, let alone salute me with that big air horn. I can't remember the last time that happened.

How lovely not to care.

West Point is coming up, little brick Tabernacle of Hope on the right, Secret Garden Nursery on the left. I love that name. Maybe I'll stop there on the way home, buy a red rose, celebrate, never mind that it's August and experts suggest you don't plant in this heat.

Watch me, I'll tell them. *I'm just getting started.*

I ease my foot off the gas pedal and creep along because the cops in this small town frown on audacious, lead-footed women, and I don't want to start this day with a ticket I can't pay. Yet.

Twenty minutes past West Point, I arrive at the gates to the sacred halls of higher learning. I find a parking place in the shade, grab my bag of books and priss my ample self to the fifth floor of Allen, right up to the president's office.

I present my credentials and make my pitch to teach writing at the university, then try not to sit on the edge of my chair and twist my hands in my lap while he thumbs through the novels I've brought.

Finally he tells me, "This is impressive. Mrs. Dufrane, I think you will be an excellent addition to our faculty."

Afterward, I walk across the campus to the Chapel of Memories. It's noon and somebody is in the tower playing the carillon, a glorious bell-music version of "Oh, What a Beautiful Morning" that makes me want to sing along.

Well, why not?

The great thing is that although I sing flat and can't remember all the words and make up new ones as I go, nobody gives me funny looks. When I get to the chapel, I sit in the attached courtyard by the fountain, lift my face to the sun and say yes. Just that. And then thank you.

Mama's napping when I get back to Belle Gardens, curled on her bed with her back to her roommate, glasses off, her lips moving as she dreams of hiding her candy. Or maybe she's dreaming of dancing in red shoes. I hope so.

Rather than wake her, I sit in her recliner and watch while she sleeps. I have all the time in the world. Shoot, I own the world.

"Maggie?" She's peering at me with one eye. Suspicious. "What's wrong?"

"I have something for you, Mama."

I go into the bathroom and bring out the dozen red roses I purchased at the Secret Garden. She claps her hands. "Ohhh."

This is not the senility of age, a gradual reversion back to childhood. This is Mama, who has never been afraid to do what children do, just let her emotions rip.

"There's more in the car. A red rosebush. Let's put your glad rags on. We're going to Mooreville to celebrate."

"What are we celebrating?"

"You're looking at 'Professor' Maggie Dufrane, gainfully employed and raring to spend."

"Well, it's high time."

She wants to wear sequins to supervise the ceremonial planting of the rose, and I pick out the flashiest outfit she has, yellow with purple, green and pink sequined flowers all over. Who cares if she looks like

Mardi Gras? Who gives a flitter if it's the middle of the afternoon and nobody wears that kind of thing till after dark?

"Why don't I pack a little bag and check you out for the night so we can get Jean and Aunt Mary Quana and have a party?"

"Okay. We'll stop at Palmer's and pick up ice cream."

"Cherry vanilla."

"No. I want to pick it out. I'm the one who told you to do this."

The side trip to the grocery store, which would take only fifteen minutes if I ran inside to get the ice cream, turns into an hour-long excursion, with Mama clomping up and down the frozen-food section on her walker inspecting every box of ice cream in the store and then stopping to tell everybody she meets about my new position, whether she knows them or not.

Here's what she says, "This is my daughter, Maggie. She's a *professor*."

I feel as if I should be passing out cigars.

Some of the people she stops listen politely and then hurry on, but some of them, perfect strangers, say, *Isn't that nice?* and *You must be so proud.* A few of them even whip out pictures of their own children and tell us about their jobs in Boise and Seattle and Albuquerque.

This, too, is a celebration for me. Watching her. Seeing the pleasure she gets in sharing small triumphs. Being thankful that she's still with me.

Exhausted from her performance in Palmer's, she leans her head against the window and sleeps the rest of the way home. The late-afternoon sun shines through the window, reflects on her sequins and puts something that looks like a halo around her.

Later, sitting in the middle of the bed with Jean and Mama and Aunt Mary Quana, the four of us eating strawberry-shortcake ice cream, Jefferson sitting on the floor beside us, ears alert and tongue drooling on the rug, I tell them about the halo.

Mama laughs till tears roll down her cheeks. "Do you reckon they really give those things out when you die?"

"Don't talk like that," Jean says, but I see something in Mama that wants an answer.

"I don't know," I tell her. "Nobody does, really, but I can't imagine anything more useless."

"Neither can I. If Saint Peter gives me one, I'm swapping it for a sun hat with a red feather."

In the midst of this conversation, Rainman calls.

"I can't talk right now, Joe. We're having a girls-only party."

"Have fun," he says. After I hang up, Aunt Mary Quana looks at me.

"Why didn't you invite him over?"

"Because I want him all to myself," I answer, and suddenly I know this is exactly what I want. An amazing encounter that wipes everything from my mind except a pair of legs tangled in the sheets, and the feeling that I'm in a world apart and nothing can happen, ever again, that I can't handle.

CHAPTER 17

Instead of talking about the weather today, I'm going to give you some advice. The sun is shining—get outside and enjoy it.
—*Rainman*

Jean and I are in the north pasture behind Mama's house, Jean taking my place behind the wheel, driving, and me taking her place in the passenger seat, happy to be striking a huge blow for freedom for myself, but praying, too.

Between silent supplications for mercy and deliverance, I'm trying not to yell, *You're going to get us all killed!*

Holding her tongue between her teeth and the wheel in a white-knuckled grip, Jean's beheading black-eyed Susans and mowing down Queen Anne's lace at forty miles an hour.

"Just take it easy," I tell her. "Slow down."

"How?"

Lord have mercy. Her driving is enough to turn me Catholic on the spot. I imagine myself clinging to a rosary, freeing my mind of the oak tree that has suddenly sprouted in our path and seems bent on doing us in.

"You remember, Jean. Just ease up on the accelerator."

"Okay." She tightens her grip, squeezes her face in concentration and presses down instead of letting off. The Jeep roars forward while Jean squeals, "Oh, lord," and lets go of the steering wheel.

I lurch sideways and grab the wheel, jerking it hard to the right just before the trunk of the oak replaces me in the passenger seat. Even my quick wits and lightning reflexes don't stop the low-hanging branches from scraping the top of the Jeep.

"Stop," I yell at Jean. "*Stop!*"

We come to a bone-jarring, teeth-rattling halt, and Jean turns to me with a sweat-slicked face and big eyes.

"It could happen to anybody," she says.

"I know."

"At least I didn't hit it."

"No, you didn't."

"I'm not sure I'm cut out for driving."

"Yes, you are. If fifteen-year-olds can learn to drive, so can you."

"Well…all right." She squeezes her eyes shut, takes a deep breath and gives a little nod, more to herself than to me. It's the kind of gesture that says this was merely a setback.

"Other than that," she asks, "how am I doing?"

Terrible. Horrible. Hopeless. These are only three adjectives that come to mind, not to mention the very real possibility that she will wreck my car and I won't have any means of transportation to my new job. Still, I'm willing to take the risk just to cut my trips to Wal-Mart in half.

"Great," I reply instead. "It'll just take you a little while to catch on."

"That's what I think." She nods and wipes her face with the bottom of her pink seersucker maternity top. "I'm going to show that Walter."

I'm scared to ask what. The last telephone conversation between them didn't go well. Between Jean's ultimatums and his stubborn refusal to be dictated to, they've come to an impasse.

Or so Jean said. But then, this is my doom-saying sister talking. I can't imagine that Walter is not as eager to be a hands-on father as Jean is to deliver a healthy baby with two stay-at-home parents.

"Why don't we take a lunch break?" I reply.

"No. While you're at work I've got to be able to drive myself around."

"Okay," I tell her. "Let's just go over a few basics again, starting with the accelerator."

"The what?"

"The *gas pedal*. That little doohickey under your right foot."

"Shoot, I knew that. I'm just nervous, that's all. Let's go another round in the pasture."

"I'm not sure my nerves can take it."

"Since when have you had nerves?" Jean puts my Jeep in gear and wrecks a perfect stand of goldenrod. "See. I'm doing fine here. All you have to do is sit over there, keep your seat belt buckled, and give me a few driving tips every now and then."

"How about...if you keep going in this direction we're going to end up in Mama's lake?"

"Whoops." Jean veers hard to the left, overcorrecting and almost smashing into a barbed-wire fence. Once she gets underway again, she shoots me an accusatory look. "Don't say a word. You scared me, that's all."

"Slow down, keep out of the lake, off the trees and away from the fence posts, and I won't say a thing. How's that?"

"You're surly, Maggie. What you need is to call Rainman and take care of your poor, neglected sex drive."

Don't think I haven't thought of it. "That's a sexist remark, Jean."

"Don't give me that feminist garbage. It's the truth. Intimacy is the world's best release for tension."

Women in my situation—meaning a certain age, alone and taking care of everybody but themselves—don't get that many opportunities.

What I tell Jean is "Just tend to your driving and I'll tend to my libido."

Jean slams on the brakes, and I can't tell whether this is deliberate or whether this is what she plans to do every time she stops.

"Look," she says. "I need lunch. Let's go inside and have some chicken salad and chocolate cake. I'm hungry."

"I thought I heard something calling my name. I might have known it was chocolate."

Jean parks beside the fence that separates her yard from Mama's pasture, and we go through the gate Walter installed and into her kitchen, which always smells like butter and sugar and whatever flavor she's decided to use in her cake that day.

The chocolate restores my equanimity, but I've never been called foolhardy, and so before we head

back to the carnage Jean left behind in the pasture—
beheaded wildflowers, flattened bushes and scraped-up
trees—I arrange an assortment of pots and pans and
serving spoons in her den as stand-ins for parts of the
car.

She masters the stew pot and the omelet pan (brake
and accelerator), the soup spoon and the cake knife
(turn signal and gear shift) from the safety of her pink
velvet wing chair without once coming close to wreck-
ing the TV and sideswiping Walter's favorite recliner.

"Are you ready now?" I finally ask. "Because if you're
not, we still have thirteen days to get you a driver's li-
cense before I start teaching."

"I don't need thirteen days, Maggie. I just need half
your confidence and somebody to believe in me. That's
all."

That explains why I'm always the one she turns to,
always the one she asks, *What are we going to do?*

"I believe in you, Jean. I know you can learn to
drive."

"It's not just driving, Maggie. Mama always believed
in you. You were the one she counted on to make the
best grades and win the awards and make something
of yourself."

"She believed in you, too. She still does."

"Yeah, but in a different way. I think she views me

as more decorative than substantial. So does Walter." She spreads her hands across her beginning-to-bulge womb. "The only thing I've ever done that's significant is get pregnant."

"Jean, that's not true."

"Name two things."

I think hard, trying to come up with an answer that will satisfy this deep need I see in my sister. Unfortunately she mistakes my hesitation for inability to answer her question.

"See…you can't even name two." She starts to cry, and I'm automatically reaching into the pocket of my jeans when something inside me tells me it's time to let Jean rescue herself.

She glances at me, fumbles in her own pockets and then goes to the hall bathroom and returns with a box of tissue. I wait until she wipes her face and honks her nose, settles into herself, and then I say, "You didn't give me time. You've done far more than two significant things, but the best are being a wonderful, caring, loving sister and daughter and a really spectacular wife. You've succeeded at being *family*, Jean, and that's worth more than holding down a high-powered job or achieving a small amount of fame."

Now I'm the one feeling teary-eyed. She hands me a tissue.

"If you think I'm fixing to make an Academy Award acceptance speech you can forget it." She peels off six tissues and stuffs them into the pocket of her maternity top. "I've got some driving to do."

I don't know whether it was the chocolate or the verbal Academy Award, but Jean's driving has improved exponentially, and after two hours of sedate navigation, she parks the Jeep in the shade of our favorite tree, an old blackjack oak. The low-hanging, swaybacked limb that made a natural swing for two little girls still holds two grown women, and we sit side by side with our shoes off and our hair blowing in the breeze that has sprung up. It's a damp sort of wind that has the taste and feel of oncoming rain, the soft, steady kind that clears gutters and washes accumulated dust off the tops of houses and cars, the kind that eases parched fields and nourishes famished gardens, the kind that feels like a jubilee.

This is how Rainman finds me, barefoot and content, my face lifted to the darkening sky and my hair springing out in moisture-fattened curls.

I saw him when he parked his pickup on the side of the road, watched as he climbed over the barbed-wire fence and headed our way. Joy spreads through me like honey.

Joe "Rainman" Jones moves with the long, sure strides of a confident, purposeful man. In jeans softened from many washings and a gray T-shirt without logo or ornamentation, he looks at home in Mama's pasture, as if he might have grown there along with the tall pine sapling he's just walked past.

When he's close enough to see my face, he waves and I wave back.

"I was delivering a handmade reproduction washstand down the road and I saw you sitting under the tree." He looks directly at me, making no bones about it.

"It's the hair," I say. "Like Moses's burning bush."

Smiling, he leans against the tree trunk, looking like somebody who would enjoy cuddling while rain patters on a tin roof and candles melt down in amber beer bottles on a red-checkered tablecloth.

He inquires about Mama and Aunt Mary Quana.

"She's moving into Belle Gardens with Mama, I'm happy to report that she got here with only one speeding ticket and no dented fenders."

Rainman gives us that endearing smile again. He inquires about Jean and she waxes motherly about her upcoming big event.

Is he too good to be true? Now that I've decided to say yes if he asks me out, I'm having all sorts of second

233

thoughts: I don't have time to waste on dates, much less an affair. I don't know Joe, not really. He must have some fatal flaw, otherwise why is he still single at his age? I'm single at my age, but I *know* why, and let me tell you, my divorce was completely justified.

But what about his? Did a wonderful woman kick him out for being unfaithful? Is this smile and concern for two women on a tree swing genuine, or is this a public persona? In private, did he treat his wife like a worm?

Or maybe he's never been married. Maybe he has such awful hidden habits that nobody wanted him. Like picking his teeth in public after a steak dinner or being rude to waitresses and bus drivers and grocery boys, or buying one ticket at the theater and then sneaking into a second movie without getting another.

Or—horrible thought—maybe he doesn't like women in that way.

But then he says, "Maggie, are you free for dinner Friday night?"

Suddenly I think of Mama, planning to roar around Belle Gardens in a wheelchair with spinner hubcaps and a Rebel flag.

"Yes," I say, just yes, and the corners of his eyes crinkle. A man with that many smile lines can't be bad.

* * *

Panic doesn't set in until he's back in his car, headed north on 371 with one long arm out the window waving.

"I can't believe I did that," I say. "A date. At my age. Lord, I won't even know which side of the bed to use. And what if he wants to keep the lights on? With these cottage-cheese thighs?"

Jean's cracking up, laughing so hard the tree limb threatens to dump both of us into the dirt.

"I don't see what's so funny. All I'm saying is that I'm out of practice. And who brings up the issue of condoms? Do I carry them in my purse or is it his responsibility? I mean, after all…you got pregnant…at your age."

"Maggie, he asked you to have dinner, not his child."

"Still, these issues might come up…eventually. Besides, what if the nursing home calls? What if Mama needs me?"

"That's why God made cell phones."

"Oh…okay." I fiddle with my hair, finger the bark on the tree limb. "I don't know what's gotten into me."

"I do. Lust…and don't you dare tell me you didn't notice how good he looked in those faded jeans."

I did. *I did.*

* * *

That's why I end up at McRae's in the mall the next day with Jean, Mama, Aunt Mary Quana and a credit card in tow.

Well, that's partially why. Sometime during the night I realized that it's not lust on my mind but *possibility* that has my head spinning. What if Joe loves stargazing and moon watching and slow bluesy ballads as much as I do, and what if Eric Clapton's "Wonderful Tonight" becomes *our* song? What if he plays a harmonica that can break your heart and not only reads poetry but also writes it? What if his mind mesmerizes me as much as his smile, and oh…what if his hands are as tender as I imagine and his kisses remind me that he's somebody I've always known—not merely as a voice on the radio—but as a lover throughout time?

I know, I know. Call me old-fashioned, but I'm just a starry-eyed romantic. And wouldn't it be lovely if there really were second chances?

But even if this date with Joe turns out to be nothing more than two people sharing a good dinner, I still want to look my best. Call me vain. Or better yet, call me Mama. She never sets foot in public without matching her blouse to her slacks and she wouldn't be caught dead in frayed underwear.

I nab a peasant skirt off the rack along with an off-the-shoulder blouse, pink and gauzy, something you might wear dancing if Andy Williams happened into town and started crooning "Moon River."

"What do you think?" I ask, and Jean immediately gives her stamp of approval to the pink blouse.

Mama comes roaring up, a die-hard shopper turned dangerous by a motor, and tosses a wisp of lace into my shopping cart.

"There. That's all Mary Quana and I could find in leopard print."

I pick up a silk thong that wouldn't hold a sneeze, let alone my backside. "Mama, I don't wear these things."

"It's never too late to start." She revs her motor and backs around the racks with the vengeance of a woman on a mission.

"Wait…Mama…where are you going?"

"To see if they have anything that's crotchless."

"Oh lord…" I say.

"She's having a ball." Jean smiles. "I'm glad you told her."

I am, too. She's as excited as she was when I had my first date. I was fifteen and gawky and Raymond Taylor was sixteen and pimply-faced, but Mama treated our outing to the movies and Dudie's Drive-In for hamburgers as if we were getting ready to exchange nuptials in the St. Louis Cathedral. I wore yellow because she said Mary Quana taught her it was a happy color, a sundress she'd made on her old Singer treadle sewing machine. And she pinned a gardenia in my hair.

"Always gild the lily," she told me. "But don't ever be anybody except yourself. Let your intelligence show, no matter who's intimidated, and don't ever tone down your spirit, no matter who gets scared and runs."

Now I follow her to the lingerie department and exchange the leopard silk *not-me* panties for a sensible white cotton pair with French-cut sides.

"I was just fooling with you," Mama says, "trying to find out what you had in mind."

"I wasn't," Aunt Mary Quana informs us. "I'm as serious as a whale in mating season."

"Hush up, Mary Quana. I'm the one giving advice here. Maggie, I don't believe in sex on the first date. Keep 'em waiting. That's my motto."

That's not necessarily my motto—I'd like to think that spontaneity enters into things of that sort—but it's certainly my intention. I don't need any more complications, and sex has a way of doing that to a relationship.

Oh, lord… I'm not ready for any of this.

"Maybe I ought to call the whole thing off," I say.

"We can't live backward, Maggie. Only forward."

Mama whizzes down the aisle with Aunt Mary Quana hard on her heels, and I trot after them.

"Mama, wait. Where are you going now?"

"To get a ruby toe ring."

"I won't wear it."

"Not for you. For me."

Don't ask. That's all I can say.

As Mama careens through ladies' wear I beckon for Jean, and the two of us join her at the jewelry counter where she's inspecting every toe ring in the glass case and asking the clerk if she can try them on.

"My feet are swelling," she says. "I don't want one that will cut off the circulation."

Jean and I look at each other, and suddenly the only thing that matters is Mama's heart and the very real possibility that each beat shortens her time with us on this earth.

It's hard not to hover over her as the salesgirl—Myrtle, her name tag reads—removes Mama's shoe and gently puts a ruby ring on her middle toe.

Mama turns her foot this way and that, admiring the sparkle from all angles. "Do you have a matching ruby for my belly button? I plan on dancing when I go through the Pearly Gates, and I want to do it in style."

Myrtle glances at us, alarmed, not sure how to react,

but when she sees us start to grin and then to chuckle, she whoops until tears roll down her cheeks.

It's healing, this kind of laughter, and it's the thing that makes me know I can go on, no matter what; it's the thing that makes me reach toward the display rack and select a pair of tortoiseshell combs set with turquoise. I work them through my tangle of stubborn curls, and when Jean sees them, she says, "Oh…perfect."

Better than hair gel is what I'm thinking. And then I'm thinking of talented, olive-skinned hands removing the combs and letting my hair fall down around my bare shoulders. Not because of lust but because of who I am—a woman passionate about all things, and not afraid to show it.

CHAPTER 18

It's going to be a clear evening, folks. Just right
for stargazing. Don't forget to look for Venus.
She's putting on quite a show tonight.
—*Rainman*

It feels strange sitting in a vehicle I'm not driving, resting my hand along the back of the seat, trying to look
casual but feeling too dressed up and a bit shy, like a
schoolgirl again, only…oh, I don't know…wiser?

"Joe, the little respites with you over the past few
weeks have helped me keep my sanity. Thank you."

"You're welcome, Maggie girl." He turns to smile at
me. "You're very lovely…especially tonight."

For the first time in a very long time I feel beautiful, sexy even, and I'm glad I wore turquoise combs in
my hair.

He takes me to Vanelli's, which I love. Wonderful

pasta and Puccini opera playing softly through the speakers, Greek statues and a water fountain, local boxer-turned-singer Paul Thorn's funky art hanging on the walls, friendly waiters and the owner himself stopping by the table to chat. It's both upscale and casual, the kind of place that says somebody likes you enough to bring you here, but it's all about relaxing, enjoying good food and having fun, being yourself.

And suddenly I can do that, relax, settle into a corner booth and be myself. I start telling Joe about keeping my radio tuned to WTUP because his easy, conversational way makes me feel as if I'm listening to a friend. I even admit that sometimes I talk back, that sometimes he's the only person in the world I can talk to.

"Wow," he says, "I guess that's why I feel as if I've known you forever."

And because I feel the same way, I ask, "Have you ever been married, Joe?"

"Yes, to a woman who was too good for this earth. She died. Six years ago. Ovarian cancer."

Love Story, I'm thinking. *Idolizing the dead.*

But Joe, who obviously reads body language if not minds, says, "We were childhood friends, and everybody always assumed we'd grow up and marry and so we did. It was an easy relationship and a wonderful friendship, and I'll always be grateful."

I tell him about Stanley and about different expectations, about trying too hard to fix something that was irreparably damaged and, finally, about leaving.

"I'm no good at playing games, Joe, and after twenty years of being married, I don't have the least idea how to date."

"Why don't we just start with pasta, and go from there?"

We go rapidly from there—to camaraderie and easy laughter to Joe's apartment on the south side of town. He leads me onto a small concrete patio and we sit in a glider just right for two.

"I'm a man of modest tastes and simple habits."

"What made you leave a big metropolis like Chicago and come to Tupelo?"

"After Lana died, I realized I'd squandered my time on cocktail parties and publicity tours and too many late nights working. If I could change one thing in my life, I'd want to go back and spend that time with her."

I blink, hard. The beautiful honesty of his answer is going to make me cry.

"That's why I came to Tupelo, Maggie. I wanted to simplify my life. I don't plan to waste another minute on the trappings of success…. I want to spend my time with people who are important to me."

"Oh…" That's all I can say.

Joe turns to me, puts his hand on my cheek and brushes away my tears. I want to wallow in this tenderness. I want to take roots in this Venus-kissed place and stay forever.

And then he reaches for my combs. "Do you mind, Maggie?"

Too full to speak, I shake my head.

Released, my wild mane tumbles down. He lets it drift through his fingers, holding it up to the moonlight so it feels as if stars are caught in my hair.

"Beautiful," he says, and then I know he's going to kiss me, just know it. And I want him to, but in my present state I don't know if I could stop at kissing. I don't want what we have between us, this tender friendship, to be changed. Not yet. I need time to savor.

So I lean slightly back and, Joe, sensing my mood, takes my hand and kisses it.

"Look at those stars, Maggie. Have you ever seen a night sky so spectacular?"

"Never." Our fingers are intertwined. "Never."

Since Mama moved into Belle Gardens, Jefferson has started sleeping by my bed. At first, I thought he is what awakens me. When a hundred-pound dog chases imaginary rabbits in his sleep, the mattress he's leaning against rocks like the deck of a ship at sea on rough waters.

But no, it's the telephone. I can hear it now, and fully alert, I grab the receiver.

"Maggie…" It's my sister.

"What's wrong?"

"Walter's coming home this evening and I want to buy a car."

"Good lord, Jean. You called at 7:00 a.m. to tell me that?"

"That's not the only reason. I want to know everything that happened last night. Blow by blow."

"Nothing happened."

"Shoot, that's no fun."

"Actually, it was lots of fun. Joe's a really great guy."

"Yeah, but did he at least kiss you?"

When I don't answer, she says, "He *did*, didn't he?" bringing me back to Saturday morning in a rumpled bed—*alone* in bed, which makes me wonder what might have happened if I'd kissed Joe underneath Venus.

To kiss or not to kiss seemed simple when I was sixteen, and now I'm wishing somebody would write an instruction manual.

Jefferson nudges my arm and starts prancing around because it's time to get up.

"Look, Jean, I've got to let the dog out. Why don't you wait till Walter comes home so he can help you pick out a car? Besides, I'm not so sure you're road ready."

"That's the whole point. You're going to give me another road lesson before we go shopping, and I'm going to *show* Walter that I'm independent and he can just pack his bag and hop on the next plane going God-knows-where. I don't care." She sniffles. "I really don't. I'll just have this baby all by myself and do my own driving."

At least she's not asking me to fix her problems, which ought to be a relief. But it's not. What I'm thinking is that I'm going to have a talk with my brother-in-law because avoiding issues is out of character for him and I love both of them and can't imagine them apart. Besides, something's obviously going on that I'm missing—more to the point—that Jean's missing.

"Things will be okay after you and Walter get a chance to talk face-to-face, Jean. He's the best man I know."

"Currently he's an ass. Are you going to take me to buy a car or do I have to call a cab?"

Women with turquoise combs for their hair and

somebody gorgeous stirring all their senses don't let their sisters dictate to them. Besides, my muses are not just whispering this morning, they're laughing and jumping up and down and doing the rhumba, and I don't intend to shove them aside for anybody.

"I'll take you, Jean, but not right now. I'm itching to write, and I'm very close to finishing a new proposal. I'll pick you up around eleven. We'll take Mama, too. Okay?"

I'd take Aunt Mary Quana, as well, but she has gone back to Atlanta to settle her affairs and bring Uncle Larry's ashes to Tupelo.

After I take care of Jefferson's business and our breakfast, I write with a freedom I haven't felt in a long time. My muses love this spirit-filled house, this peaceful farm, these beautiful memories of almost being kissed under the magic light of Venus.

Jean and I are in the Jeep with her at the wheel, creeping down Highway 371 at forty miles an hour. She's steady, she's careful, she checks her rearview mirrors and doesn't fiddle with the radio. Even when cars start lining up behind us and the driver of a red Ford pickup toots his horn, she plows sedately onward.

"At least I'll never have to worry about you getting a speeding ticket," I tell her.

"You've got that right."

When the pickup truck roars past, horn blaring and driver shaking his fist, my normally well-behaved sister lifts her middle finger and shoots him the bird. Then she glances over at me and grins.

"Hormones," she says. "Mine are on the rampage. There's no telling what I'll do next."

"Well, just make sure the next driver you flip off doesn't weigh two hundred and fifty pounds. I don't think I could whip him in a road brawl."

By one o'clock we're at the Ford dealership, which is owned by Lawton Wilson, an old friend of Mama's. When he spots us getting her out of my Jeep, he comes outside to help and then leans over and kisses her hand.

"Victoria, light of my life, what can I do for you?"

"You can kiss my other hand, and then you can give my daughter Jean the best bargain in the showroom or else you can kiss my foot."

Obviously he believes her because he gives Jean a deal on a maroon Explorer that all of us agree is rock-bottom. She wants me with her to sign the paperwork, and we go into Lawton's small glassed-in office while Mama sits outside the door in a chrome-and-black-leather chair. The wraparound windows allow me a perfect view of the showroom, and when I see Mama moving slowly across the polished floor, leaning heavily on her walker, I start to race to her rescue. *Bathroom*, I'm thinking.

But I'm wrong. Her destination is on the other side of the showroom, shiny as Dorothy's ruby-red slippers and just as magical. At least to Mama. It's the car of her dreams, a Thunderbird convertible, white leather interior, designer hubcaps, chrome hood ornament poised for flight.

A young salesman in an earnest seersucker suit and a trustworthy navy tie hurries over. I can't hear what they're saying, but I can guess because he opens the car door for Mama and helps her inside. She puts her hands on the wheel and sits there, smiling and nodding. *Yes*, I imagine her thinking. *I can go to New York in a car like this*.

By the time we finish with the paperwork, Mama is back in her chair, humming under her breath—probably some bawdy Broadway number—unaware that I've seen her wishful journey.

And all too soon it's time for the part of this expedition I've been dreading: watching my sister get behind the wheel of a car and drive home alone. Mama quickly scotches that idea.

"I'm riding with Jean."

Before I can protest, Jean says, "Mama, I don't want to risk that."

"Flitter. You're fixing to be driving my grandbaby around. You can use me as a guinea pig." With amazing upper-body strength, she grabs the seat belt strap and hoists herself into the Explorer.

"Maggie," she says, "shut this door and follow Jean. I've got to get home and pick out furniture. I'm moving into my private room tomorrow."

Three days earlier than I expected. I wonder what Mama did to accomplish that. I hope it was something positive such as sweet-talking Belle Gardens' administrator, but it might as easily have been a shouting match with her roommate over stolen chocolate.

I'll never ask. Some things are best left unknown.

The fifteen-minute drive to Mooreville takes thirty. Even after Jean parks the Explorer and helps Mama inside, I sit in my Jeep under the magnolia tree, taking deep breaths and telling myself that this is the hardest letting go I'll have to do, watching my sister cast aside her dependence and brave the highways alone. Well, not alone. Even worse. Carrying my niece or nephew. And Mama.

When I finally go inside, I realize the fallacy of my thinking, for Mama is clumping through the house on her walker, saying, "I'll take my recliner and my bed and my collections, but I don't care what happens to that old oak rocking chair. I never did like it," while Jean follows along behind taking notes.

Seeing me in the doorway, careful-faced and still, Mama stops. "Maggie, do you think you can hang my Japanese fans in my room at Belle Gardens?"

I don't know what I say, but whatever it is satisfies Mama because now she's in the bedroom going through her jewelry box, telling Jean what she wants to pack and what she plans to save for her granddaughter.

"Mama, we don't know the sex yet."

"Well, I do. And I want her to have this pearl necklace. It's real. Write that down, Jean."

I know these are merely possessions, insignificant, really, when you think about life and our fragile hold on it and what our time here on earth means. But I can't bear to watch Mama picking what she will take and what she will leave behind. I can't bear the thought of walking into her bedroom, devoid of its cherry four-poster and the eighty-five Japanese fans on the wall.

Why that vision is more painful than walking in and seeing it empty of Mama, I don't know. Maybe it's the finality of this act that won't let me stand upright, that makes me hurry into the kitchen and sit on a straight-backed chair, holding Mama's faded apron in my lap.

All these months I've kept her things exactly in place, waiting for the day when she will come home again.

She still might is what I tell myself, but Truth is whispering in my ear. I close my eyes and say please. Maybe it's a prayer, maybe it's hope. Maybe they're the same.

CHAPTER 19

Good morning from WTUP. We're broadcasting from Coley Road where we're predicting the biggest furniture market Tupelo has ever had and plenty of sunshine to keep everybody happy.
—*Rainman*

Here I am on Highway 371, driving behind a caravan that feels like a funeral procession, the death of a spirited, Mama-directed era. There's a big void in me, and right now I can't think of how I'll fill it.

Up ahead, Mama's sitting upright in the passenger seat of Jean's new car, beginning the last leg of her journey—backseat driving, I'm sure—while my sister carefully follows the lead car of this caravan. Walter's in front pulling a U-Haul with the furniture Mama's taking to Belle Gardens.

She spent the night at Jean's even though it was the

253

first time Walter had been home in weeks. I think Jean deliberately planned it so she wouldn't be alone with her husband. He looked strained and fatigued this morning, and Jean looked…I don't know…triumphant somehow, as if there's something growing in her besides a baby. Courage and determination and some of Mama's piss-and-vinegar sass.

Well, maybe I have some of that myself. Although I'm living out of suitcases and boxes and the only dog in my life is Jefferson, who can't decide whether to go completely bald in his old age or hang on to his hair, I've come a long way since I raced down this highway to Mama's rescue. My sister's driving (my doing) and pregnant (I claim no credit!) and I have a lucrative job and a delicious male friend.

The mere thought of Joe makes me tingle. I wish I had kissed him when he took the turquoise combs from my hair. Maybe reclaiming my sexuality would have put me one step closer to being center stage of my life. Or smack dab in the center.

But, look on the bright side—at least I'm no longer playing a bit part. If I had three hands, I'd reach over and pat myself on the back.

Belle Gardens comes into view, but I don't let myself think about endings. Instead I unload eighty-five

Japanese fans from the back of my Jeep and go inside
to start hanging them in Mama's new private quarters.

"I'm going to have the best-looking room here," she
says. "Everybody's going to be green with envy.... Not
there, Maggie...to the left. And wait till Laura Kate
and Annie see it. They're going to wish they were
here."

Sitting with her swollen feet propped up, yellow
shirt bagging over thin arms and sunken chest, and col-
lapsing blue veins crisscrossing her hands, Mama
makes you think she's lucky.

See? my angels whisper. *See?*

"Maggie, can you help me outside for a minute?"
Walter's standing in the doorway with sagging shoulders and bags under his eyes. Not the face and posture
of a man happy to be home.

Under the guise of unloading an end table from the
U-Haul, he says, "Do you know what's wrong with
Jean?"

"You need to ask her."

"She's barely speaking to me, much less anything
else. I need your help, Maggie."

"All I know is, she's anxious for you to be home. Because of the baby."

"That's what's scaring me to death. We're too old for

255

this. Do you know the percentage of miscarriages for people in our age bracket?"

"Don't think like that."

"I can't help myself. I keep thinking this isn't real, something's going to happen. I mean…Jean's already talking about the best kindergartens and colleges, for Pete's sake, but I can't let myself start believing I'm going to be a father because too much could go wrong between now and February."

"You need to say that to Jean."

"How?"

There he stands—intelligent, successful, big-hearted and helpless—a giant of a man who has always protected Jean from every harm, brought low by the thought that he can't control events, that nature and fate and the gods of the universe have a plan of their own, a design that might be imperfect.

What he needs is a sister to hold his hand, a friend to say everything's going to be all right, and a mother to tell him to buck up. He even needs a weatherman on the radio to predict lots of sunshine's coming his way. What he gets is a big hug from his sister-in-law.

"Tell her exactly the way you told me, Walter, and I can guarantee you that everything's going to be all right."

"You think?"

"I know."

What do you know? I sound just like Mama. When I go back inside to resume hanging fans, I notice that the rose garden outside Mama's window is filled with yellow roses. Like sunshine.

When I get home, I walk through the echoing house. It's too quiet here. Even when I turn on the radio and hear Rainman's voice, I still feel as if I'm alone in the middle of a desert.

This is dangerous thinking. I try to perk up my spirits with a long bubble bath, a nice purple caftan that swings around my bare ankles, a spritz of Jungle Gardenia that makes me feel like a sultry woman. I brush my teeth with Close-Up. Mouthwash added. Fresh breath guaranteed. In case somebody wonderful wants to kiss you. In case somebody wonderful even knows you're alive.

Jefferson trots behind me to Mama's mostly empty bedroom where I settle into the rocking chair she hates, pick up the phone.

"Mama…is everything okay?"

"Don't you have anything better to do than call me? Like watch *Golden Girls* reruns? I've got company here."

"Male or female?"

"None of your business."

"Mama...I'm coming right over."

She giggles. "I had you going there for a minute, didn't I?"

"You always do."

I put down the phone, stare at it, wait for it to ring. I don't know if my sister's silence is good news or bad. Good, I'm hoping, because Jean always calls me when something goes wrong.

Or, she used to. My entire landscape's changing and I haven't learned how to decipher the map.

I take Jefferson outside and stand a while on the front porch watching the stars. Venus looks as if she's hanging from the lowest point of a silver crescent moon. I love it when that happens. This letting-go feeling inside me doesn't hurt as much.

When I sit on the porch swing, Jefferson plops beside me and I tuck my bare feet against his warm fur to watch the best show in town. But it would be twice as good shared.

Suddenly I feel like a traveler coming to a big fork in the road: I can take the paved, well-known highway or I can veer to the left onto an unfamiliar winding road, destination unknown. Veering to the left, I go back inside and pick up the phone.

"Joe, I moved most of Mama's furniture into her private room today, and I don't want to be by myself."

"You don't have to, Maggie. I'll be right over."

I wait for him on the front porch, still barefoot. When he hugs me, we're both vividly aware that I'm naked beneath my caftan.

"Are you okay?" he asks.

"Yes, but better with you here."

He still has his arms around me, and I hold on to him and breathe, simply breathe. Cocooned, safe, I lean into him and feel how his body welcomes me. This is no polite, obligatory embrace, but one where you know the giver understands your need.

Right now, my greatest need is for comfort, and Joe gives just that until I make the first move to break contact.

"I have something for you, Maggie. Wait here."

He bounds down the front-porch steps, and comes back with a rocking chair, hand-carved roses on the handles.

"I thought you might be needing this."

"How wonderful." I sit down and put the chair in motion. "It's exquisite. All I need now is a four-layer chocolate cake and somebody to massage my feet, and I'd be in heaven."

"I can't do anything about the cake, but I think I can take care of the rest."

He pulls a wrought-iron chair opposite me, puts my feet in his lap and, one by one, massages my toes. By the time he's working on the balls of my feet, I feel every nerve in my body, every bone, every ounce of blood pulsing at my temples and singing through my veins.

Moonlight and starlight wash over us, and the brief flicker of a firefly lights the darkness. I don't know how long we sit there, his hands sending all kinds of signals through the soles of my feet. I don't wear a watch because I like to think that I control my time and not two little mechanical hands ticking off minuscule numbers I can no longer read without glasses.

"Maggie, I have the day off tomorrow. Will you go with me to Pontotoc to an estate auction?"

Rusted-out lawn chairs and battered-up suitcases and old, musty clothes smelling of mothballs and neglect. Used tires against a tree, weeds in the roses and a rope swing, sad and raveling. Heat and mosquitoes and the microphone turned too loud so there's no escaping the grating, insistent voice of the auctioneer.

Funky and fun, I'm thinking, and I say yes.

"Great." He stands up, kisses my cheek. "I'll pick you up around ten."

When he flashes his pickup lights at me, I wave, still in the rocking chair. I may not be able to get out until next Tuesday. I am jelly-legged and flushed, wide-awake all over and ready to explode. But in a good way, a *very* good way.

I put on my hopeful yellow sundress, pluck a gardenia and tuck it in my hair. Then I worry that I've gone over the top, that I look like somebody expecting too much. Joe arrives in a Mustang convertible, vintage, and I'm glad I'm wearing yellow, glad that the scent of gardenia follows me when I move.

"Hmmm. You smell nice," he says, a man who notices such things. "Do you mind the top down?"

"Not at all." My flower is securely pinned, and even if it blows off, I like the idea of being a woman who leaves gardenias in her wake.

The Victorian house is on the south side of Pontotoc, with lots of shade and an apple orchard so old it looks as if Johnny Appleseed planted it. Joe takes a handmade quilt out of his trunk and stakes out a place for us under the shade of a blackjack oak.

The crowd buzzes with excitement as floor lamps and marble-topped tables and crystal vases are trotted out one by one and sold to the highest bidder. *Is this what happens when you die, when you move on to another place? Strangers pawing over your possessions?*

Melancholy catches me high under the ribs, and for a moment I can barely breathe.

"Maggie?" Joe touches my face, sees my tumult. "I'm sorry. I didn't think how closely this would hit home. We'll leave."

"No...wait."

The auctioneer is hawking books now. A little girl with a sun-streaked ponytail and gap-toothed smile walks by, clutching an armful of Nancy Drew mysteries as if they're King Tut's treasures. "Can I read them now, Mommy? Can I?"

"I'm fine." I say this to Joe and mean it. This is not a one-note life we're living. I know I can bear the pain; now I must learn to embrace the pleasures.

"You're sure?"

"Absolutely. Maybe we'll discover something wonderful."

Joe bids on a leather-bound copy of Shakespeare's sonnets, and the hubbub of the crowd vanishes as he opens the yellowed pages and reads Sonnet 29, which ends: "For the sweet love remember'd such wealth brings/That then I scorn to change my state with kings."

I close my eyes and fall into his deep voice. When I open them, he's smiling.

"Hungry?"

"Hmmm." In more ways than one. I'm blushing and not caring who sees.

"Wait right here."

I'm feeling so languorous I couldn't move if a stampede of African elephants headed my way. I stretch out on the quilt, close my eyes....

"Welcome back, sleepyhead." My head is cradled in Joe's lap and he's smiling down at me.

"I can't believe I did that." *Oh lord.* I feel old, like one of those women who falls asleep in front of the TV.

"I'm flattered, Maggie. It means you trust me."

"I do. Completely."

Amazing, all the things you can learn about a man if you take things one step at a time. If I had used Joe merely as a way to satisfy a newly awakened libido, I would never have known that he's the kind of man who packs Kentucky Fried Chicken and cloth napkins in a wicker basket, that he's the kind of man who carries a harmonica in his pocket. And—oh joy!— that he's the kind of man who plays the blues harp in such a soulful way it breaks your heart.

It's dusk when we leave, a lovely, honeysuckle-scented evening that feels important, that makes my skin tingle and my heart race. Joe takes the long way home, a meandering drive down the Natchez Trace that allows time to stop by the side of Davis Lake underneath a lethal moon-Venus conjunction.

We watch the stars in heart-thumping silence, and when he leans close, I slide into his arms, drunk on the heady scent of honeysuckle, the taste of his mouth, and amazement.

It's the kind of amazement that won't let me sleep and, after Joe takes me home, I turn on my laptop and fall into the fantasy world of unicorns and magic.

By the time I come out of my imagined world, it's three o'clock and I've finished a new proposal. With white candles and a brimming-over heart, I go outside and pay homage to the Universe, to the perfect order of stars and moon and to the spirit of women everywhere who still believe in miracles.

CHAPTER 20

It's going to be mostly sunny today with patches of light showers in the early afternoon. If you like being prepared, take your umbrella. If you enjoy the surprise of life, kick off your shoes and sing in the rain.

—*Rainman*

Although I didn't go to bed until three-thirty, I'm up at eight, feeding Jefferson, poaching an egg and keeping one eye on the clock. At exactly nine o'clock—ten eastern time—I grab the phone and dial Janice Whitten.

"I have a new proposal."

"Great. Send it."

"It's not another revision of my mystery. It's a story that came to me and wouldn't go away. Fantasy with a touch of sci-fi."

She pauses, and I wait, hardly breathing, worrying at a fingernail I chipped on my keyboard. A lifetime and one ragged nail later, she says, "I can't wait to read it, Maggie."

I hang up, do a little jig, race into town, mail my proposal by Federal Express, swing by Belle Gardens to see Mama, then go home and collapse. The phone wakes me at two o'clock.

It's Joe, calling to thank me again for a lovely day and to see how I am.

"Great," I tell him. If I felt any better I'd be turning Aunt Mary Quana's cartwheels. But I have much better activities than she does planned for the moon.

On Monday, I drive to my first eight o'clock class at MSU. It's six-thirty and I'm barreling down Highway 45 while the rising sun puts on a show just for me. I own the world.

Soybean and cotton fields stretch for miles like fat green and white ribbons, interspersed with open pasture full of grazing Black Angus cattle. I feel a vaulting freedom driving alone this time of morning, a wonderful sense of accomplishment as I pull into Hardee's in West Point for a hot sausage and biscuit. I know exactly where I'm going and what it took to get here, and I'm proud.

Leaving behind the town that gave birth to the blues of Howlin' Wolf, I start to get nervous. I haven't been in the classroom in ten years. What will I say? Will I tell them everything I know about writing in the first fifteen minutes, and then run out of anything to teach? Can I make them understand that writing is more than words on paper, more than ideas set down for others to read? Can I inspire my students to write with wide-open hearts and split-apart souls, with color and truth and no-holds-barred passion?

Oh, I must. *I must.*

I'm scared when I park, but triumphant, too. Faculty, the sign on this parking lot reads. That's me. Maggie Dufrane. University faculty. Determined, purposeful and independent.

I step out of the Jeep and take a deep breath. Even the air feels different. Bursting with ideas and dreams. Energizing.

Lee Hall is just ahead, the oldest building on campus, old brick and stately columns and a million steps leading through the double doors. Four months of this and I can say goodbye to the saddlebags on my hips as well as the hole in my bank account. *Hallelujah.*

I climb the steps, trying to look like I belong, and my cell phone rings.

"Maggie…I just wanted to say good luck on your first day."

"Thanks." This is the first time I've heard from Jean since we moved Mama into her private room. A record. "How in the world have you been?"

"I'm good," she says, which tells me exactly nothing.

I could wring her neck. Here I am, headed to my classroom and I'm going to have to spend the next fifty minutes worrying and wondering about my unusually taciturn sister.

"For Pete's sake. You know I've been worried about the two of you. What's going on?"

"I'm not kicking Walter out, but we've still got a lot of stuff to work through."

"You will, Jean. He loves you and the baby, too."

I push through the doors—heavy, ornate, important-looking—and enter a long hallway that smells of lemon wax and ancient knowledge and the brashness of youth.

I turn my cell phone off and go into room seventeen, where twenty students are sitting in rows wearing faded jeans, MSU T-shirts and expectant expressions.

"Hello, I'm Maggie Dufrane," I tell them, and suddenly I'm a writer, teacher, mentor, wise earth mother who wants to tuck all these young people under her wings and tell them not to be afraid, to be themselves, that's what I want them to learn. Be brave. Write freely. Live fully. But most of all, be kind and hug somebody. There's too little kindness in this world.

My first-day-teaching jitters vanish, and I take my place behind the podium and begin the unexpected, giddy process of falling in love—with my students, with teaching, with life.

On the way home, I stop at Belle Gardens to tell Mama about my great day. I find her in the beauty shop in tight rollers, face pink from the heat of an old-fashioned hooded hair drier, flipping through a *House and Garden* magazine dated June 1999.

When she sees me, she shoves the hood back and announces, "This is my daughter Maggie. She teaches at MSU."

I don't remind her that everybody in this room has met me. Instead I stride into the middle of the tiny shop like somebody important, like somebody Mama's proud of, and say hello.

"Maggie, you've got to settle an argument. I told Mert you didn't have to reach around behind and nearly pull your arms off to hook your bra in the back. You could hook it in the front and then turn it around.

She didn't believe me. Said it would get twisted. Tell her."

"Mama's right. She's been doing it that way for years. And I'm fixing to start."

"See. I told you." Mama gives Mert a smug look. "And she's a university professor."

While Mama gets her hair combed, I tell her about my day, about Jason who sits on the front row and has a natural talent for writing, about Stephanie whose enthusiasm for life is infectious, about Gabe whose big smile makes this world a better place.

"My office overlooks a small courtyard with a fountain. You know how I am about my writing space. And I'll have plenty of time for that, too."

"You are where you belong," she says. "I knew it all along."

On the way to her room, Mama's so slow that I walk beside her with baby steps and an anxious heart. When she sinks into her recliner, it takes a while to get her breath back.

"That hall gets longer every day," she says, and I don't say anything. I can't.

Finally I remember the Reese's peanut butter cups in my purse. "I brought you something, Mama." There's a Dollar General Store two blocks from Belle Gardens.

I can stop there every day on my way back from MSU and get her a small treat.

"Good. I'm glad I don't have that old hog rooming with me anymore. I'm going to eat every one of these, myself." She unwraps one, and I stand by the window looking at a yellow rose in the garden while she eats.

"Maggie…" There's something in her voice that demands attention, and I move to sit in the wing chair across from her. "I want you to have my house."

She has to stop for breath while I struggle to keep my thoughts from showing on my face. *Mama is never coming home. The house will never be the same. Jean and I will never go there again and find her sitting in her recliner issuing edicts about everything from chicken soup for winter colds to the difference between vicious rumors and informative gossip.*

"Mama, you don't have to think about things like that."

"You might as well hush because I've already called my lawyer to put the deed in your name."

"But Jean…"

"Has a house and knows exactly what I'm doing, but even if she didn't approve, I wouldn't give a flitter. It's mine and I'll do what I want to with it."

Suddenly I see that little house with pots of red geraniums on the front-porch steps, a little patio out back with a water fountain and a wrought-iron table just right for breakfast alfresco and laptops.

"Mama, I'm overwhelmed."

"You and Jean take what you want and sell everything else. Or give it to Salvation Army and Goodwill. I don't care. Build a big bonfire in the backyard and burn it, if you want to. I have everything I need right here. Besides, I don't know what they'd do without me."

"But, it's not as if you'll never be coming home again."

"Flitter, I don't want a bunch of old junk to have to worry about. When I visit *your* house, I'd better not catch you trying to turn it into some sort of mausoleum. Slap some red paint on the walls. Put in a garden tub. Get a king-size bed. Sounds to me like you're going to need it."

"What has Jean told you?"

"That's between me and Jean and gatepost. Have you had sex with him yet?"

No, but I'd like to. "Why don't I just put an announcement in the church bulletin?"

"While you're at it, you might want to put one on the Belle Gardens bulletin board."

"What for, Mama? I have you."

"Yes, you do. And you'd better not forget it."

* * *

As I drive back to Mooreville and start thinking about dismantling Mama's house, the wonder of having my own home fades. I can't do it. Certainly not alone.

Suddenly it occurs to me that I'm not alone, that I don't have to do this by myself. I have my sister, my brother-in-law, my friends. I even have Rainman.

My cell phone rings and his number flashes across the screen.

"Do you read minds? I was just thinking about you."

"Maggie…" Oh, this doesn't sound good. No lilt. No *I was thinking about you, too* tone. "I'm headed out of town for a few days."

Where? Should I ask him, or is that nosy? Does one kiss give me the right to know?

"I just wanted you to know. I'll call you when I get back."

Is he the kind of man who is scared off by the thought of intimacy? Does he excel at friendship and run at the first sign that the woman wants more?

And I do. I do.

There's only one good thing I can say about his phone call: it knocked everything else right out of my mind. That just goes to show the state I'm in. A woman ready to be ravished. Period.

* * *

I don't hear from Joe all week, and I'm frustrated. I didn't even ask him how long he'd be gone. It's a relief to be so busy I don't have time to think about him. At least not much.

And I don't think about the house, either, because transforming it is an act of finality. And I'm not ready to eradicate the last bit of evidence that Mama lived—and reigned—here. I can't.

On Friday when I stop by Belle Gardens with a bag of Hershey's Kisses for Mama, she says, "Take me to Lowe's."

"Why?"

"Because I'm going to pick out paint for you."

"You might not pick what I want. It's my house."

"Exactly."

That night, I call Jean over for a family conference. I invite Walter, too, because he's still in town—the longest stretch I've ever seen—but she says he has work to do in his home office.

"I'll fix supper," I tell her.

I go into Mama's kitchen—it's impossible to think otherwise—and start making spinach salads. Because stress always demands butter, I make a peach cobbler and check the freezer to make sure I have some vanilla ice cream, real cream and plenty of sugar.

I set the table with Mama's blue plates and bowls, run my hands around their cool rims and decide to keep them, because I can't imagine the kitchen without them. Jefferson interrupts his doggy nap under the table, trots to the front door and stands there wagging his tail. It must be Jean.

"How do dogs do that?" I say as I let her in.

"Yeah, I know," she agrees because she's seen him do it a million times, standing in front of the door, wagging his tail or growling, never mind that he can't see who's there. "Do you think they read minds?"

"Maybe."

We go into the kitchen, sit down to eat and discuss dispensation of Mama's worldly goods, and don't make it through the salads.

I fumble in my pocket for tissue and hand her one, but she has already found one in her purse.

"If you've got something with butter and sugar, you'd better get it. It's going to take a lot of comfort to get me through this," she sniffs.

"Me, too."

I dump our half-eaten salads into the garbage, scoop huge servings of ice cream over mammoth portions of still-warm peach cobbler, and we don't say anything for

275

a while. It takes a lot of concentration to eat melt-in-your-mouth-buttery-crusted cobbler without getting tears mixed up with your ice cream.

Finally, I say, "I don't want to sell her things."

"Neither do I. I'd feel like Judas taking thirty pieces of silver."

For once, over-dramatization is the only truth. We look at each other, mute, and then Jean holds out her empty bowl for more dessert. I refill mine, too, and finally, powered on sugar and fat, we walk through the house, making decisions that pelt stones at our hearts.

Mainly, I make the decisions on what to keep and what to give away because now Jean's crying so hard she can barely see.

"You'll want Mama's rocking chair for the baby's nursery," I say, and she nods. "The Swiss music box, too."

There's a satisfaction in knowing that another generation will hear the same "Blue Danube Waltz" Mama used to play every night when we were children. She'd tuck us in bed, wind the music box and wish us sweet dreams.

Now I take the music box off the shelf and wind it while Jean and I sit cross-legged on the floor, holding hands and remembering sweet dreams.

* * *

After she leaves, I go to the front-porch swing. The moon and stars are turning in a bravura performance, so bright they light Mama's front yard with spotlight intensity. Correct that. My front yard.

I'm sitting here in my white nightgown, grateful for the privacy of country acreage that allows this kind of indulgence. If Horton and Hattie happen to look out their front door and glance this way—which is highly unlikely because they always turn off their lights at nine and don't turn them on again until six the next morning—all they'd see would be a glob of white. And maybe not even that unless they're using binoculars.

Jean's at home now, and I picture her curled up in her pink wing chair talking to Walter about supervising the Salvation Army and Goodwill trucks that will haul off Mama's furniture. She volunteered his services and I didn't say no, didn't feel the least bit cowardly. If I've learned one thing since Mama began her battle with congestive heart failure, it's that I can't do this alone. Family matters. Friends count. Sometimes even the kindness of strangers can help us get through the day.

John Donne was right about no man being an island. I think I'll assign his famous Renaissance "Meditation XVII" to my students. That's an important lesson, and all of us should learn it. *We're not in this alone*.

Jefferson whines at the front door. I tell him, "Coming boy," and get up to let him out. He does his business and then settles beside my chair, sprawled in the grass, his big head resting on my feet. This feels right. I am finding my center, connecting to the stars, opening myself to something vast and amazing, some new understanding that makes my soul sit up straight and say, *Now I see*.

Sighing as if he's also privy to new insights, Jefferson stirs and I feel his warmth on my feet, feel them putting down roots so deep they'll hold no matter how high the wind and how fierce the storm.

Early Saturday morning, Jean and I leave for Home Depot before the trucks arrive.

"The trick is to let go, move fast and move forward," I tell her.

I reach for a Ralph Lauren paint called buckskin, a rich golden-yellow that looks like sunshine pouring across the walls.

"What do you think of this for my office? I want a happy, look-alive color. And for my bedroom, rose, not prissy and feminine but something both soft and bright."

"Romantic," Jean says.

"Exactly."

"When are you seeing Joe again?"

"I don't know. I don't even know where he is or if he's coming back." I tell her about his phone call.

"Good grief. He's probably just taking care of business. Men don't tell everything the way women do. Don't worry, Maggie. He'll call."

"You think?"

"He'd be a fool not to."

One of the beauties of having a sister/friend like Jean is that when I'm blue she can always make me feel better. My sass is back as I prance to the Jeep and pull it in front of the store to be loaded. I'm a woman full of possibilities—all of them wonderful.

After we leave Home Depot, we go directly to Belle Gardens so I can show Mama the paint chips.

"You didn't get an old-turd brindle-green for that dining room, did you?"

"No. Ming-red."

"Good. Design consultants always try to talk you into green, tell you it's restful and soothing. Who wants to fall asleep while they eat?" She clumps over to her window on her walker to hold the paint chip in the light, and stands there a while, nodding and smiling.

"I like it," she says. "I'm going to get a hat that color

so the next time the Baptists come here to sing I can give everybody something to think about instead of all that caterwauling."

"Mama," Jean scolds. "You don't have to go to those programs if you don't like them."

"Flitter, I'm the belle of the ball down here. They wouldn't know what to do without me."

Would we?

As soon as I get home, I put on faded jeans, an old blue T-shirt and start painting. Bedroom, first. With luck, I'll finish before evening, and tonight I'll fall asleep in a soft glow that feels like sunrise.

Alone. Why hasn't Joe called?

I won't let myself worry about it. I'll keep moving forward, a woman who knows exactly what she wants and where she's going.

The phone rings and I almost don't answer it, figuring that by the time I climb off the ladder it will have stopped, anyway. But what if it's Mama? What if it's Joe?

"Maggie?" It's my Rainman, and I'm so relieved I have to sit down. "I just got back from Chicago. My brother wanted to sell some family property on Lake Michigan, and I drove up to talk him out of it."

"You have a brother?"

"Yes. And a sister, too. I want them to meet you."

The promise of his words steals my breath, and he says, "Maggie? Are you still there?"

"I'm here. Painting. My bedroom."

"I'll come over and help you. I like working with my hands."

I have forty minutes to think about Joe's hands and what I'd like him to do with them, and by the time he arrives with a sack of Wendy's burgers and a six-foot ladder, I'm ready to snatch off his soft-looking, faded T-shirt.

He touches my face, which gives away my thoughts. "You're hot, Maggie."

If only he knew. Maybe I'll tell him. Somewhere between dinner at Jean's and ice cream in the hayloft, I've turned into a wanton vixen. Before this night is over maybe I'll turn into a seductress, too, a woman who doesn't wait for a man to make the first move, a woman who just reaches out and takes what she wants.

"Why don't we take a break and eat?" He unwraps the burgers, hands one to me, and we sit cross-legged on the floor while he describes his family—a baby sister who is a nurse and a single mother to five-year-old twin boys, and an older brother who is an avionics engineer with a lawyer-wife and no children.

Afterward, we paint, and by the time he puts the last brush of rose across the top of the windowsill, the moon is shining through, impossibly bright.

He climbs down from the ladder, turns on the radio to a station whose DJ promises a night of jazz and blues, then puts down his paintbrush.

"The bedroom's finished," he says.

"I know."

Tucking a stray curl behind my ear, he says, "May I have this dance, Maggie?"

"I'm not much of a dancer."

"I don't think that's what matters here."

At first I'm clumsy and self-conscious, afraid I'll step on his feet. Then he pulls me close and I feel his body's rhythm, relax into it. Suddenly I'm dancing, not at all the clumsiest girl in Miss Femura Wright's dance class, but Miss Gracie Smallwood waltzing to the promise of "Moon River."

I tell Joe about her, about her pink chiffon dress and her rhinestone tiara.

"Thank you," he says, and I don't have to ask for what? I know. It's about hope that two people our age can still discover the joys of old-fashioned romance.

I lead him to my bed and remove the drop cloth, never mind imperfect body parts and full-cut white cotton panties that would be more at home as a flag of truce than an instrument of seduction.

We sink deep into the feather pillows and my comforter folds tentlike over us as Joe touches me with hands that know how to carve a rose.

Suddenly I'm sixteen and giddy, racing through the meadow with the sun in my hair and goldenrod at my feet, happy to be alive, filled with hope and dreams and the absolute assurance that anything is possible.

Yes, I'm thinking. Just that one word. *Yes*.

Sunday morning, I wake up with Joe in my bed, propped on one elbow looking at me. "Good morning, sleepyhead."

"Oh, hey..." The sun pours through the window, and in its unforgiving light I'm self-conscious. Women my age depend on the enhancement of lipstick and blush, flattering blouses and soft lights. I'm plagued with the unsettling thought that not only am I out of practice, I'm past my prime and will never be the kind of woman who sets men's hearts aflutter with dewy appeal at seven o'clock in the morning.

Joe kisses me, then pulls the covers over our heads. All of a sudden I'm Julia Roberts, with legs long enough to wrap around Texas. I'm Marilyn Monroe with enough sex appeal to bring powerful men to their knees. I'm Maggie Dufrane who wallows in wrinkled sheets without a single thought about flaws and the passing of time.

CHAPTER 21

Good morning, folks. This is Rainman Jones,
coming to you live from WTUP. There's going to
be plenty of sunshine today, the kind of day that
makes you want to burst into song. 'You were
meant for me; I was meant for you....'
—*Rainman*

Rainman's back at the station, barely arriving in
the nick of time, I'd think, considering our morning;
Walter flew to New York this morning; Jean and I are
on the way to Belle Gardens for eleven o'clock devo-
tionals.

"Maggie, if you're out there listening, that was for
you."

Jean turns up the volume and says, "Maggie, that's
you."

I'm beside myself to finally be the kind of woman who gets special songs dedicated to her on the radio.

Mama's waiting for us in a new red hat Jean got for her at Parisian's. *Ostentatious* is a mild word for it. Wide-brimmed and important-looking with both flowers and feathers floating across the top, it's just the kind of thing Victoria Lucas would pick.

"Do you think everybody will notice?" she asks as we escort her into the dining room where the Baptist choir is warming up with "I Come to the Garden Alone."

"How could they fail, Mama?" I wish the choir had picked a perkier number, maybe a jazz rendition of "Down by the Riverside," but nothing can mar my morning. Shoot, nothing can mar my life.

After church, we help Mama into the car. This takes a while. Each day now takes its toll. But to see her, you'd never know—the way she holds her head, as if she's royalty doling out favors to an adoring public, the way she still snaps out sassy retorts and is the first one to laugh at herself, even when she stumbles.

After I've folded her walker and finally settled her into the car, she says, "Before we eat, drive by the Ford place. I want to take a look at that car."

If it weren't Sunday afternoon, I'd whip inside and ask a salesman if we could take the red Thunderbird for a test drive. Instead I park as close as I can get so Mama won't have to leave the Jeep.

"Wouldn't I be something in that car?" she says.

"Yes, you would. But you know what, Mama? You're something anyway."

"Maggie, now that you're in your house and Jean's pregnant, I want you to cook the family's Thanksgiving and Christmas dinner, carry on the tradition in my style."

Nobody can carry on in her style, but I don't tell her this. Instead I ask if she will supervise the preparation of the dressing.

"Flitter, as long as I'm still kicking I'll be the boss of everything."

After lunch, we take Mama home and head to my storage unit. I unlock the door and start rummaging through stacked furniture and boxes. The first thing I find is the box of outgrown clothes.

"I can't believe I paid to save these." I slash my red pen across the box, marking it for Salvation Army. "And these…lord." Two boxes of craft magazines. I never did crafts when I had a huge house and plenty of time. Why did I ever think I'd use them in my cramped apartment?

I know why. I was still clinging to old ideas of myself. When I was married to Stanley, I imagined I would be the kind of woman who decoupaged flowerpots and knitted pot holders and tie-dyed aprons. Now I know I never was that kind of woman and never will be.

There's my blue stool, my hand-blown glass perfume bottle with the tasseled bulb spritzer, and, oh, my satin high-heeled slippers with the feather trim. That's who I am. The kind of woman who sits on a velvet stool in ostrich plumes while she sprays the inside of her knees with Jungle Gardenia.

I set these items aside to take with me and Jean plops onto the velvet stool and says, "This is Walter's last business trip abroad. He has a few more loose ends to tie up and then he's starting his own consulting business here."

"That's great news." Lines of fatigue are etched around her mouth, and if perkiness were motor oil, she'd be about a quart low. "Isn't it?"

"Yes, I'm thrilled. It's just that…well…he'll need a lot of good business contracts and it makes sense for him to have business partners, people who know everybody in Tupelo…."

"For Pete's sake, Jean…get to the point."

"Walter needs an accountant in the firm…and a lawyer. So we've been having business meetings with

Stanley and Sandra Martin…the lawyer…his new girl-friend."

I sit down on a dining-room chair. Hard.

"Are you mad at me?" Jean says.

The effort of holding back is too much, and I open my mouth and howl with laughter.

"Good lord…" Jean gets up from the stool, her energy restored. "I *told* Walter you wouldn't care, but he said, 'No, we'd better keep it to ourselves a while.'"

"Shoot, doesn't he know there are no secrets in this family?"

"I'm glad you said that. I saw a car at your house when I drove Walter to the airport this morning. I want details. Tell all."

"Except that," I tell her, giving her a mischievous look. "As Mama says, it's between me and Joe and the gatepost."

"I know what I'm getting you for your next birthday."

"What?"

"Condoms."

"Jean, you're awful."

"So are you." She links her arms through mine. "What do you say we stop by Dairy Queen for a banana split? To celebrate."

When I think of the long journey from April to

August, and how far I've come, I want to stand on top of a tall building and shout, *See? Some spirits can't be broken.*

"You know what I'm thinking?" I ask Jean.

"What?"

"That I'll invite Stanley and Sandra to Thanksgiving dinner. In some ways, he's part of this family."

"What about Joe?"

"Joe, too." And always, if I have anything to say about it.

On Monday, I stop by JCPenney on the way home from MSU to get new lace curtains. I'm hanging them when the phone rings.

"It never fails," I tell Jefferson. "The next time I want somebody to call I'll just climb onto the stepladder."

The caller is Janice Whitten. "Maggie, this fantasy is the best thing you've written in a long time. It's riveting, honest and full of life."

"You like it, then?"

"Like it? I *love* it. I'm offering a contract."

Relief and gratitude flood through me, and all I can think is *I'm a writer. I really am a writer.*

"How soon can you finish it?"

The way I feel right now—reborn, my creative well

brimming over, the road ahead of me as clear as the lake in back of my house on a sunny summer day—I could write three hundred pages in the next three days and still have time left over for dancing.

We work out the details and, after I send Jefferson scuttling under the bed with my whoops and war dance around the house, I call everybody I know to share the good news—ending with Rainman.

He brings stargazer lilies and a patchwork quilt, and lying under the stars we celebrate in a way that's infinitely better than cream-filled doughnuts and far less fattening. Afterward, with the night breeze drying our damp skin, we find the constellations and then plan a trip to Chicago to meet his family and Thanksgiving dinner with Mama, Jean and Walter, Aunt Mary Quana, Stanley and Sandra.

"And anybody else you want to invite," I tell him.

"Let's start with that guest list and go from there."

On the seventy-mile drive to MSU the next morning, I imagine where Joe and I might go from here. And the possibilities are limitless.

Gabe and Stephanie see me striding across campus, wave and fall into step beside me.

Maybe I'll invite them to Thanksgiving dinner, too. Maybe I'll invite all my students, everybody in Lee County, the whole world. That's how wonderful I feel.

* * *

Driving back to Tupelo, my first paycheck in my pocket and a contract in the works, I stop by the Ford dealership and go inside. The Jeep is old and paid for and costs very little to insure. I have medical insurance through the university, no house payment, a small utility bill, and miniscule grocery and household maintenance bills.

"May I help you?" the salesman asks, and I just smile.

Two days later, the Lucas family heads to the hospital for a momentous occasion—to find out the sex of Jean's baby. At least, we hope we will.

"Ultrasounds are never one-hundred-percent reliable, especially this early in the pregnancy," her obstetrician tells us as we move through the long hallway toward the room where Jean's ever-expanding womb will be explored for the family—Walter, nervous in navy-blue suit and discreet tie; Jean, Madonna-like in a pink hospital gown; Mama, festive in her red hat; and me…well, *sassy* is the only word to describe me, especially since I'm waiting to spring my own surprise.

Jean grabs my hand. "You're going to take Mama back, aren't you?" Although I nod, she goes on, "Walter and I are flying to Sedona afterward, and she'll want to go somewhere and celebrate."

"I know," I say, but Jean doesn't seem to hear me.

"Somewhere nice. I was thinking Ivy's. That's where we'd take both of you, except our plane leaves at five and—"

"Hush, Jean," Mama says. "You're going to make the baby nervous and she'll turn her back and we won't know a thing about her till she's born."

"It might not be a girl, Mama Lucas," Walter cautions.

"Flitter, I know what I'm talking about."

This is a slow-moving parade, this family celebrating the advent of a brand-new little person coming into our midst. Between the orderly pushing Jean in a wheelchair and Mama on her walker, it takes us twice as long to get to the room where we'll witness a miracle.

Everybody except Walter waits outside. When Mama and I are finally ushered into the too-cool room where Jean is laid out on the table like an offering to the gods of the technology surrounding her, we see the first wavery outlines of the fetus on the monitor.

"Can you believe that? Ten little toes and ten little fingers," Walter says, as if his is the only baby ever conceived with the proper number of digits.

"Oh…look." Jean lifts her head for a better view. "It's a boy."

Mama clomps over and plants herself squarely in front of the monitor, blocking everybody else's view. We don't say a word—we hardly even breathe—while she stands there nodding her head, the feather on her hat bobbing like a wild redbird learning how to fly.

"It is *not*," she finally says. "That's the umbilical cord." She puts her hand on the screen, right over the tiny hand of the unborn baby Victoria. "Hey there," she says. "Hey there, precious one."

Then she turns to us, eyes snapping and hat askew. "That's my granddaughter, you're talking about. You'd better not let her hear you call her a boy or she'll pitch a hissy fit."

"Just like her grandmama," I say.

"You've got that right," Mama says, and then does a little hula inside her walker.

I've parked my car in one of the hospital's disabled slots, the permit I use because of Mama displayed on the dashboard.

"Maggie, where's your Jeep?" She comes to a halt in the parking lot. "Somebody *stole* it."

"No, they didn't, Mama. *That's* my car."

For once, she's the one rendered speechless. She walks slowly around the Thunderbird, running her hands along its sleek red sides, taking her handkerchief out of her purse and polishing the hood ornament. Claiming her dream.

Finally she says, "I'm glad I'm wearing my red hat. It matches."

I help her into the passenger side, stow her walker in the trunk and then let the top down.

"Hang on to your hat, Mama."

We glide out of the parking lot, and she waves at everybody she sees. Any minute I expect her to yell, *Look at me! This is my daughter, she's owns this car.*

"Where's your Jeep?"

"At home. I kept it for hauling stuff like furniture and barnyard fertilizer. And for the times Jefferson wants to go on trips with us." I turn south on Gloster, but I'm not heading toward Belle Gardens. "Do you feel like taking a spin, Mama?"

"If I felt any better I'd be turning cartwheels and shooting poots at the moon," she says, and here's what I'm thinking: the doctor said one to seven years, but with that kind of courage, I'm betting on seven.

I skirt around the city, backtrack and head downtown, driving slowly, up every major street and through the subdivisions, too, because Mama's still waving, and I want to make sure everybody in Tupelo sees her. When she spots the mayor coming out of city hall, I swear she sends him the beauty-queen wave.

"Drive by Laura Kate's," Mama says. "I want to make sure she sees me in this car."

As we leave the city, I notice that the countryside looks different, brighter somehow, the green of leaves and grass, the pink and yellow of roadside wildflowers more hopeful, the road I'm traveling clearly defined.

"Maggie, can we go to New York in this car?"

"We'll go next summer, Mama. Aunt Mary Quana can go with us. We'll buy red scarves that match and drive all the way with the top down."

"If it doesn't rain."

"It won't."

And even if it does, I've learned how to open my umbrella in sudden showers, navigate through monsoons and wear hip waders in floods.

"It wouldn't dare," I add, a woman completely in charge. I picture the universe sitting up and taking notice.

Three friends, two exes and a plan to get payback.

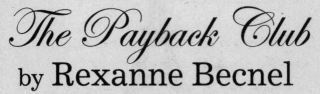

The Payback Club

by Rexanne Becnel

USA TODAY BESTSELLING AUTHOR

HARLEQUIN®

N_{xt}e

Available January 2006
TheNextNovel.com

HN26TALL

Artist-in-Residence Fellowship—
Call for applications

She always dreamed of studying art in Paris,
but as a wife and mother she has had
other things to do. Finally, Anna is taking
a chance on her own.

What Happens in Paris

(STAYS IN PARIS?)

Nancy Robards Thompson

HN26TALL

Available January 2006
TheNextNovel.com

Mothers, sisters and other passengers

Novelist Maggie Dufrane's mama is the Mississippi queen of drama. When her sister Jean drops a shocker on the family, Mama thinks it's the best gossip she's heard all year. But it's up to reliable Maggie-the-family-chauffeur to fix things...again.

Driving Me Crazy

PEGGY WEBB

A woman determined to walk her own path

Joining a gym was the last thing
Janine ever expected to do. But with
each step on that treadmill, a new
world of possibilities was opening up!

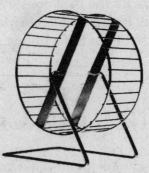

TREADING LIGHTLY
ELISE LANIER

What happens when new friends get together and dig into the past?

Ex's and Oh's
Sandra Steffen

A story about secrets, surprises and relationships.

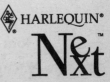

Sometimes the craziness of living
the perfect suburban life is enough
to make a woman wonder…

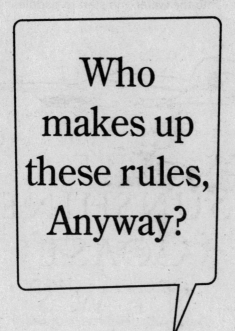

Who
makes up
these rules,
Anyway?

BY

STEVI MITTMAN

HN301ALL

Since when did life ever tell you where you were going?

Sometimes you just have to dip your oar into the water and start to paddle.

THE
SUNSHINE
COAST
N E W S

KATE AUSTIN

Available February 2006
TheNextNovel.com

HN32TALL

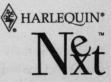

HARLEQUIN®

Next